Praise for

# THE RETRIEVAL ARTIST SERIES

One of the top ten greatest science fiction detectives of all time.

*—io9*

The SF thriller is alive and well, and today's leading practitioner is Kristine Kathryn Rusch.

*—Analog*

[Miles Flint is] one of 14 great sci-fi and fantasy detectives who out-Sherlock'd Holmes. [Flint] is a candidate for the title of greatest fictional detective of all time.

*—Blastr*

If there's any such thing as a sci-fi *CSI*, the Retrieval Artist novels set the tone.

*—The Edge Boston*

What links [Miles Flint] to his most memorable literary ancestors is his hard-won ability to perceive the complex nature of morality and live with the burden of his own inevitable failure.

*—Locus*

A nifty series cooks on.

*—Booklist*

Rusch does a superb job of making the Retrieval Artist books work as fully satisfying standalone mysteries and as installments in a gripping saga full of love, loss, grief, hope, adventure, and discovery. It is also some of the best science fiction ever written.

—*New York Times* bestselling author
Orson Scott Card

Readers of police procedurals as well as fans of SF should enjoy this mystery series.

—*Kliatt*

What links [Miles Flint] to his most memorable literary ancestors is his hard-won ability to perceive the complex nature of morality and live with the burden of his own inevitable failure.

—*Locus*

Part CSI, part Blade Runner, and part hard-boiled gumshoe, the retrieval artist of the series title, one Miles Flint, would be as at home on a foggy San Francisco street in the 1940s as he is in the domed lunar colony of Armstrong City.

—*The Edge Boston*

Rusch defines emotional and intellectual cores in her stories and then plots the most fruitful and gorgeously panoramic orbits around them.

—*Wigglefish.com*

# Praise for
## *The Recovery Man's Bargain*

Rusch's story is a powerful and engaging exploration of the pitfalls of moral compromise.

—*SF Gospel*

...has a Golden Age vibe...(an) impressive tale.

—*Tangent Online*

# Praise for
## *Recovery Man*

Rusch creates instantly sympathetic characters in a convincingly fragmented future wherein the petty mistakes of one culture translate to heinous crimes in another.

—*Publishers Weekly*

This high-tech detective story, part of the Retrieval Artist series, has hard science fiction, a complex whodunit and a fascinating look at alien bureaucracy. All the elements for an entertaining story are here: well-drawn, believable characters with frailties and flaws, credible scientific theory, and authentic-feeling settings.

—*RT Book Reviews*

## The Retrieval Artist Series:

# The RECOVERY MAN'S BARGAIN

## A RETRIEVAL ARTIST SHORT NOVEL

## KRISTINE KATHRYN RUSCH

WMG
Publishing

# The Recovery Man's Bargain

Published 2012 by WMG Publishing
www.wmgpublishing.com
First published in *Analog SF*, January/February, 2009
Cover art copyright © Philcold/Dreamstime
Book and cover design
copyright © 2012 by WMG Publishing
Cover design by Allyson Longueira/WMG Publishing
ISBN-13: 978-0-615-70162-2
ISBN-10: 0-615-70162-0

**WMG Publishing**
www.wmgpublishing.com

# The RECOVERY MAN'S BARGAIN

## A RETRIEVAL ARTIST SHORT NOVEL

# 1

THE FIDELIA PLANT GAVE OFF ITS OWN LIGHT. HADAD Yu recognized it by the faint bluish purple luminescence that shone like a beacon in the fetid swamp. His hands shook.

His entire future stretched before him, in the guise of a flower half the size of his thumb.

Three years. Three years and a dozen false leads had brought him here, to this thousand-kilometer swamp between Bosak City and Bosak's only ocean. He was 632 kilometers in, at the lone stand of colesis trees his scanners had been able to find.

The colesis trees, warped and twisted by the lack of light, bent over him like adults over a small child. He wasn't sure if a larger man could have fit into the space. He was wiry and thin, something that usually worked to his advantage.

Like it did now. He wouldn't have seen the tiny bluish purple light if he hadn't already stepped inside the circle of trees.

Now the key was to remove the plant without alerting the supporting vines or killing the delicate flowering mechanism. His client was paying for the flowering capability, not for the fidelia itself.

It was a miracle he had found the thing. Yu was beginning to believe that flowering fidelias had gone extinct centuries ago. He was willing to keep searching on all the inhabited worlds in this small sector because the client was paying expenses and because she was in no hurry to get the fidelia.

He had worked two hundred other jobs while working on this one, fattening his bank accounts and upgrading his ship. Besides, as he had explained to the client, work on the fidelia had to go slowly. Because of the demand for the flowering version, he had to work alone. Any lead would send an assistant to another client, offering to find a flowering fidelia for one-quarter Yu's price.

Personally, he had thought the quest for the flowering fidelia an insane one. A plant easily grown in a hothouse had become an interstellar sensation among the very rich. Why? Because the flowering version couldn't grow in a hothouse, and because old legends claimed that the flowering fidelia cast a light so beautiful that nothing compared to it.

Yu wasn't sure it was the most beautiful light he'd ever seen, but it was soft and delicate, with a strength that took his breath away.

Part of the light's beauty came from the flower itself. The flower peeked out of the fidelia like a bashful woman. Its petals were silver, the leaves around it a faint veiny green. The light seemed to come from above, illuminating the flower's center.

He crouched near the flower, careful not to touch it. The old writings said that a flowering fidelia remained in bloom for sixty nights, but would die if removed from its habitat. The only successful removals had taken sections of the habitat, and even then, the flower's bloom only lasted a week after the removal.

Fortunately for him, his client didn't want the flower for the bloom or its particular light. She wanted it for its genes, hoping to do some hybridization so that all the captive, non-flowering fidelias could be reborn into something much more beautiful.

Part of Yu's pursuit these last three years had included study with several botanists, who taught him how to work with delicate plants in difficult environments. He hadn't even started his search for the flowering fidelia until he could remove the non-flowering variety from its home tree without killing the tree, the vine, or the fidelia itself.

Even though he had the skills, he was nervous. The wrong touch and the light—that precious light—would go out forever.

He slipped on his breathing mask. Usually he hated the damn things—they smelled of cleaning chemicals and recycled air—but he was relieved to put it on now. The stink of the swamp—a combination of rot, feces, and burning sulfur—was supposed to fade the deeper he had gone. But it hadn't.

He removed his collection kit from his travel pouch. The kit had delicate steel cutters as well as plant resealers.

He wrapped the container around his waist, but he didn't open the lid yet.

The bit of colesis tree inside was different than the trees in front of him. The wood was dry for one thing, and it wasn't twisted.

The few botanists who specialized in non-flowering fidelias stressed that the attached vine would need a similar kind of colesis tree or it would recoil, maybe even kill the fidelia itself.

He didn't dare toss the bit of colesis he had brought with him—no one knew if the trees, which had a hearty (albeit primitive) communications system through the roots, could communicate when they weren't root bound.

He didn't want to slog three days back to the skimmer he'd left on the closest mapped island. In that skimmer, he had four more kits as well as two empty containers.

But he couldn't risk the journey. He could travel the three days there and back, only to find that the flower was gone.

He really didn't want to camp here until the fidelia flowered again.

Because that was the other problem: No one knew how often the blooms appeared.

He had to trust that colesis trees communicated only through touch—whether it was in the root system or through the water that stained his boots. The studies of colesis trees focused mostly on whether that communication ability indicated sentience.

Like so many similar studies of other plants and creatures found in the known universe, this study proved that the colesis tree had no sentience at all. Yu had a hunch that some future crisis would show that the colesis tree really was sentient in some form or another, and the Earth Alliance would work to guard the species.

But for now, what he was about to do was perfectly legal—even if it did make him squeamish.

He stepped back in the muck and examined the fidelia's colesis. The tree was nearly lost beneath the thickness of the vine wrapped around it. He'd seen the vines surrounding colesis trees being grown in large domes, but those vines had been as thin as his fingers.

This one was thicker than he was. The little hairy tendrils seemed like whiskers or some sort of vine protection device.

He wasn't even sure his steel tools were strong enough to chop through the vine, let alone the tree.

But he couldn't use a laser scalpel. Nor could he just blast away. He had to work carefully and quickly so that nothing would sense the injury before he was done.

So he turned to one of the colesis trees behind him. A separate vine wrapped around the nearest tree. That vine was thick too.

Yu slipped on his membrane-thin gloves and gently, ever so gently, used his thumb and forefinger to touch the edges of the vine.

It was softer than the vines he was used to, and the exterior was thin. So thin, in fact, that he was afraid the very presence of his fingers would rupture it.

Which presented a whole new problem. He didn't want the vine to disintegrate on him.

He made himself take a deep breath of chemical tinged air. He had to relax. Something could go wrong. And what was the worst case?

Worst case was that he would move on, see if he could find another flowering fidelia. It might take months, it might take years, but he would be all right.

He hadn't notified his client of this find yet, so she had no expectations of success. She had warned him that he would only get one chance at getting a flowering fidelia for her. She gave him a time limit—eight years— to find one. If he found one and failed to bring it to her, or worse, killed it in the process, she wouldn't pay him. Worse, she would tell all her very rich friends that Yu was a cheat, a liar and an incompetent.

She would make certain he never had work within the Alliance again.

Her threats terrified him almost as much as the big payout attracted him. That was one reason he took so many lessons in botany. Another was that he usually avoided such large payouts. Usually, he found small items for people who had lost them.

Lost was a loose term. Perhaps it was better to say he recovered items for people who did not have them. Why they didn't have those items wasn't his concern. Sometimes those items were legitimate heirlooms, truly lost or stolen. Sometimes the items were merely things that the client wanted and couldn't have, things that might, in the strictest sense of the word, belong to someone else.

Yu's recovery policy was simple: He never asked the client for proof of ownership for an item he went after. He always assumed the client owned the item and somehow misplaced it. Such a defense had worked when he'd had a run-in with authorities, most of whom couldn't touch his clients—either because the clients had too much money, too much clout, or weren't Alliance members.

This client, Magda Athenia, had both money and clout, and she had opted out of the Alliance decades ago. She claimed to be retired, but she kept her hand in a score of businesses.

Yu had researched her before he had taken on the search. First, he wanted to know if she had the kind of money she claimed she had. She did. Then he wanted to know if she honored all agreements she entered into, even handshake deals. So far as he could tell, she did. Never once had a case been brought against her in any existing court for breach of contract. All employees, past and current, had nothing bad to say about her.

He did not take the research much farther. Some of his colleagues—the ones who specialized in large payouts like this one—often tried to find out why the client wanted an item. Sometimes the client was a collector. Sometimes the client needed the item to enhance his business. And sometimes he wanted it to humiliate a rival.

Yu didn't care why his clients wanted their items. To be truthful, his clients weren't that important to him.

The importance—for him at least—was the hunt. If he were more of a collector himself, he would gather his own items. But he didn't have a permanent home, and he loved to travel light.

So he used the clients as a way to keep himself fed, and as a way to keep himself active and searching. He got paid when and if he delivered.

For the past twenty years, if he took a job, he delivered.

He hadn't missed.

Not once.

It was that statistic that had brought Athenia to him in the first place. The high end Recovery Men (and all but few in this profession were male, for reasons he never fully understood) had a failure rate of about fifty percent. Some of that wasn't their fault. Sometimes they found themselves pursuing items that didn't exist. Even with the legend factor taken out of the equation, though, the high end Recovery Men failed twenty-five percent of the time.

Now, standing in this swamp, facing away from the flowering fidelia but still bathed in its light, he wondered why he had ever taken this case. It certainly wasn't for the money. He had known from the start that he might not get paid.

It was the challenge, the near impossibility of the idea.

The hunt.

At least one Recovery Man had failed before him. That made this particular hunt even more tempting.

Yu took a deep breath, tasting chemicals. He hadn't failed yet. Even if he killed this flowering fidelia, he wouldn't fail.

The very idea soothed him, calming his nerves.

Then, before he had a chance to think, he whirled toward the flowering fidelia, steel blades flashing. With one quick movement, he slashed a circle in the colesis tree—a big circle that cut through the vine as well as a large section of the tree's interior.

With one hand, he tipped the container upside down, dumping the dried, straight colesis into the murky water. With the other hand, he pried the circular cut off the standing colesis. As the first colesis hit the water, he moved the container, catching the twisted colesis, its vine, and the precious flowering fidelia.

The light continued to pour from the flower.

So far, it seemed, the vine and the fidelia didn't sense anything wrong.

He slammed the lid on the container and shoved it into his travel pouch. Then he scurried out of the copse of trees.

The Alliance might believe that the colesis weren't sentient, but he wasn't going to gamble his life on that fact. He ran through the swamp, hitting the summon button for the skimmer.

He stopped a few kilometers away to make sure the container was stowed properly. When he was certain it was, he took out his scanner, checking for other colesis trees. There were, he remembered, half a dozen that stood alone between here and the swamp's entrance.

He was going to do everything he could to avoid them.

He was going to do everything he could to survive.

# 2

THE SKIMMER REACHED HIM TWELVE EARTH HOURS after he had found the flowering fidelia. He was never so happy to see a machine in his entire life.

The skimmer was long and flat—a costly rental that he never would have splurged for if it weren't for the fact that Athenia paid for all expenses promptly. The interior formed only when a passenger was on board. As he stepped inside, the once-flat top of the skimmer became a dome made of clear black material. He gave the skimmer verbal orders to find the quickest way back to Bosak City where his own ship was.

He went into the captain's quarters—a fancy name for the skimmer's only sleeping compartment—removed his clothes and showered not once but five times, finally giving up when he realized the stench of the swamp probably wouldn't leave his nostrils until he physically left the area.

Then, and only then, did he go back into the main cabin and open the travel pouch.

The container still glowed with that bluish purple light. As long as he saw that, he knew that the flower was still alive.

He slumped in the pilot's chair. Relief filled him, even though he knew the journey wasn't done. He still had to get the flower to Athenia.

The question was when did he notify her? If he waited too long, the flower might die of its own accord. If he did so too soon, he might lose his one chance at success.

What mattered most was timing.

If he could find out where Athenia was staying and how far it was from Bosak, then he would know if he had time to make certain the flower lived.

He couldn't make that determination on the skimmer. He might not even be able to make it on his ship. The *Nebel* had a good computer system, one that could tap into the systems of most ports, but he wasn't sure if it would work with Bosak's port.

The place truly was as far away from the Earth Alliance as he liked to go.

Since he could do nothing except wait, he closed his eyes. He needed the rest.

He knew that leaving a planet with contraband material could be tricky. It could be even trickier when that contraband material was a living plant.

He needed to be alert when he faced Bosak's version of space traffic control.

The last thing he needed was yet another arrest.

# 3

HADAD YU HAD BEEN ARRESTED FIFTY-SIX TIMES. Forty-nine of those arrests had been within the Earth Alliance and three of those forty-nine had been so serious he thought he was going to have to spend decades of his life in prison.

But he'd managed to slip away each time. Most of the lesser charges he could talk his way out of. The seven times he'd been arrested outside of the Alliance, he had used his clients—or his clients' lawyers—to free him.

But the three serious charges had taken a lot of smarts, a lot of bargaining, and in one instance, a case of bribery that was even more illegal than the crime he'd been charged with.

As a young man, he'd looked on the arrests as part of the game.

Now, though, he hated them—not just for the time they wasted, but for the luck he was using up. Some day, he knew, that luck would run out.

He thought of all of this as he sat on the bridge of the *Nebel*, waiting for permission to leave Bosak City. Each of the three ships ahead of him had received permission, only to be stopped just inside the dome. Inspectors boarded and hadn't emerged for at least two Earth hours.

The *Nebel* was four times the size of those other ships. It was a cargo vessel that he had purchased five years ago with the proceeds of his last big job. It was a Gyonnese ship, which meant that it had a lot of wonderful equipment that was so unusual most Earth Alliance inspectors had never seen it, even though Gyonne was a long time member of the Alliance.

Yu hadn't followed all Alliance protocols either. The cargo bays probably weren't as clean as they should have been. If a ship went through standard Alliance decontamination procedures, then it also got a thorough inspection. He didn't want the interior of his ship on any port database.

One of the things that had saved him in the past was that his ship didn't fit any known model. Inspectors didn't realize that the interior of the ship was larger than it appeared. Nor did most know how many separate environmental systems it had.

So if an inspector tested the air for contaminants in, say, the bridge, he'd get a completely different reading than he would in one of the cargo bays.

Usually, though, Yu didn't have such sensitive cargo. He had to keep the flowering fidelia near him. The plant needed all the atmosphere he could provide. He had it in a darkened room off the bridge itself, a room he kept as humid as possible, and he hoped that would be enough.

So far, the fidelia still glowed. He hoped it would for another day when he could finally—safely—contact Athenia.

*Nebel*, said an official voice. *Prepare for interior scan.*

Yu let out a breath. He had already protected this deck from the scan by creating a shadow deck, one that would look good on most equipment in most ports. He hoped it would work here.

*Scans show you have living material near the bridge that is not on your manifest. Please explain.*

Yu cursed silently. He could try to tough it out or he could pull his only bargaining chip. He didn't have time to research Bosak law, so he didn't know how closely it was bound to Alliance protocol.

If Bosak law followed Alliance protocol, he had no shot, not with the contaminants this ship had been exposed to.

He waved his hand over the console. His movement had switched on his side of the communications array.

"Space Traffic," he said. "I have a special license which allows me to carry items not listed in the manifest. I am sending that license to you now."

He passed his fingers over a different part of the console, then sighed. Either the port would reject the license outright or it would take time to examine it.

The license claimed that he carried top secret cargo that had already been screened by various government regulators. It was legitimate. It would hold up to examination.

The problem was that the license had come from Athenia's company. Now he would have to notify her, whether he was ready to or not.

The silence on the other end both encouraged and worried him. If they were going to board him, they would do so in the next few minutes.

He sat very still, watching the monitors. Then the digitized voice returned.

*Your license is in order. Thank you for spending time in Bosak City. You are cleared to leave.*

He bowed his head, letting relief course through him. If he had been arrested this far out, he had very few options and even fewer bargaining chips. Athenia had been one of those chips, and he wouldn't have been able to use her twice.

Then he straightened his spine, passed his hand over the console to initiate the take-off procedures, and let the ship do the rest.

He had to contact Athenia before Bosak City did.

He had to let her know that the flowering fidelia was on its way.

# 4

Fortunately Athenia picked a rendezvous spot only an Earth day away from Bosak. She had been excited to hear that he finally found a flowering fidelia, excited enough to pay his current expenses and to promise him a bonus if the thing bloomed for longer than the expected week.

Yu finally got some much needed sleep. He sprawled on the large bed he had indulgently placed in the captain's cabin, secure in the knowledge that in a few hours the fidelia would no longer be his concern.

But it felt as if he hadn't been asleep more than a few minutes when the ship woke him up. An image floated above the bed—the *Nebel* surrounded by a dozen ships, some above, some below, some to the sides—all of them blocking his way.

"Is that a threat of something to come?" he asked the ship. "Or is that really happening?"

"It's really happening," the ship said. The seductiveness of the voice, which he had programmed for solo trips, suddenly seemed inappropriate.

"Have they contacted us?" Yu sat up, rubbed his hand over his face. He felt bleary. How long had it been since he slept so deeply? A week? Two? A month?

"No contact," the ship said.

Yu's stomach clenched. That wasn't good. He got out of bed and pulled on some clothes. "Can you show me a better image of the ships?"

"This is how they appear," the ship said.

Yu wasn't sure what that meant. Was that how they appeared when the ship scanned them or was that how they appeared through the ship's various portholes?

"I'd like to see the ships' identification," he said.

"They have no markings."

He was shaking now. The *Nebel* had no weapons, because he so often flew the large cargo ship solo. Instead, he had opted for great speed and all sorts of interior shadowing technology, which allowed one section to appear to be something it wasn't.

"The shadowing technology is on, right?" he asked.

"It is," the ship said, "but we have not been scanned."

No contact, no scan. His heart was pounding. "Have we been boarded?"

The ship did not answer. His mouth went dry. He walked to the door of his cabin and waved his hand over the locks.

They didn't open.

"Ship," he said again. "Am I the only one on board?"

The image of the *Nebel* surrounded by a dozen ships vanished. A woman's face appeared in front of his door.

She had vertical blue lines running from her forehead to her chin, making it seem as if her face had been taken apart in sections and put together badly.

"You will be alone in a few moments, Hadad Yu," she said. "We have let you know our presence as a courtesy. And we want to give you our thanks."

"For what?" he asked, although he was afraid he knew.

She didn't answer. Instead she smiled and the image vanished.

He tried the door again. It didn't open.

"Secure channel YuPrivate," he said, giving one of the many codes he had programmed into the ship.

"Yes?" The ship's seductive voice had vanished.

"Open the goddamn door to my cabin," he said.

It slid open and he stepped into the corridor. The air had a slightly metallic odor that was unfamiliar—something the environmental systems hadn't yet cleaned out.

"Am I the only one on the ship?" he asked.

"Yes," the ship said.

He cursed. He thought of grabbing a weapon, but decided against it. There was no point. If the images he had seen were accurate, there were too many people surrounding his ship. A weapon would only make him seem desperate and might, in fact, put him in danger.

Instead, he hurried through the empty corridor to the bridge.

It was empty. A small black holo-emitter sat beneath the pilot's seat. The woman's image, looking almost real, filled the chair itself. She had to have sat there at some point to get such a clean image.

She was shapely, her body stronger than most that spent a lot of time in space. She had muscular legs and powerful arms, visible through the ripped top she wore. The image smiled at him. The blue lines on her face were less disturbing when the rest of her body was attached.

"Hadad Yu," she said. "The Black Fleet thanks you. While we will not return the flowering fidelia to you, we are forever in your debt."

The Black Fleet.

He had thought they were a myth, something made up to scare Recovery Men and other solo travelers. The stories were wide and varied, but they all boiled down to one fact:

When a ship was filled with valuable cargo, it would find itself at the mercy of the Black Fleet. Sometimes the Black Fleet killed the occupants; sometimes it stole the ship.

"You're in *my* debt?" he said to the holoimage.

The woman smiled. The image had been programmed to respond to simple—and expected—queries.

"We would not be here without your expertise. We have used that expertise many times without your knowledge. After a while, even we feel guilty at not paying for a service." Her smile grew. "And now, thanks to you, we can afford to be magnanimous. So we honor that with a one-time debt, payable in anything except the return of the flowering fidelia."

She touched a hand to her forehead, and the image winked out.

He wanted to pick up the box and fling it across the bridge. But he knew better. The box could provide him with some answers. It also was the only proof he had of this debt. Not only that, he suspected the box had a way to contact the Fleet built-in.

If the rumors about the Black Fleet were true, then the rumors about its attitude toward debts were true too. The Black Fleet honored all debts, considered them life debts, and as such they were quite valuable.

He stared at the box. He supposed he could tap it for its secrets. Maybe the box itself provided him with the answers he needed—not just to the Black Fleet itself, but also how its members got on board his ship.

But he wasn't going to examine the box now. Instead, he walked to the room beside the bridge.

The door swished open to reveal complete darkness. The flowering fidelia's light had gone out. He wasn't sure what was worse: the idea that the flower had died or the idea that the Black Fleet had stolen it from him.

"Lights up ten percent," he said.

They came up slowly, revealing an empty room.

The container, with the fidelia inside, was gone.

He nodded. Then blinked at an unaccustomed moistness in his eyes.

"Ship," he said. "How long has the fidelia been gone?"

"Two hours," the ship said.

"What about the Fleet surrounding us?"

"It was here for thirty minutes."

"Why didn't you wake me?"

"You left no such instructions," the ship said.

He opened his mouth to argue, then paused. While it was true he had left no instructions to wake him during that nap, it wasn't true that the ship had no instructions about waking him.

It was supposed to wake him whenever a ship was in the vicinity, or if someone or something was trying to communicate with him.

The ship certainly should have awakened him if someone tried to board.

"Can you show me what the intruders did after they entered?" he asked.

"Certainly." The ship displayed the same image that it had when it had awakened him—all of the ships surrounding the *Nebel*. Then it showed him the face of the woman. He suspected, if he hadn't waved it off, he would have watched her reappear in his chair as well.

They tampered with his systems. Now he had to figure out if they had tampered before or after they boarded.

"May I see what happened after they left?" he asked.

"They have not left," the ship said.

His stomach clenched. All of the messages suggested that they had left. Everything they had done suggested they were long gone.

He walked to the nearest porthole and looked out. He saw no ship. He went to the next porthole. No ship.

They had tampered with his systems. His ship still believed it was surrounded.

He needed to get around whatever blocks they had put into his shipboard computer. He tried a different question, one the Black Fleet probably wouldn't think of.

"Is there some kind of trail that suggests that ships have left the vicinity?"

"Yes," the ship said. "More than a dozen ships have departed this area in the last 24 Earth hours."

A dozen ships, like the ones on the screen.

"When did they leave?" he asked.

"I cannot tell from the trails, but they should thin within twelve hours. They have not."

"Can we follow them?"

"You have programmed in a rendezvous point and time. If you wish to make the scheduled point and time, then we cannot follow."

He didn't want to see Athenia. "Even if the ships are close?"

"They are not close. I can track the trails past this solar system. To chase them would mean you would miss any possibility at the rendezvous."

"Can we find them if we follow?" Yu wasn't sure what he would do if he caught up, but he was contemplating an attempt.

"I do not know."

"Did the ships leave at the same time?"

"Judging by the trails, they did."

"And head in the same direction?"

"Yes," the ship said.

"Can you make a map of these trails for me and plot a possible trajectory based on their directions?"

"Yes."

"Save that for me," he said. "I might need it."

## 5

HE LOOKED AT THE MAPS THEMSELVES, THEN AT the images of the ships. If the images were accurate, he would have had no chance of going up against them even if he had weapons. Every one of those ships could destroy his.

They got the better of him and he knew it.

So he headed to the rendezvous point. Athenia was the only chance he had. Her employees were scattered all over the known universe. She might be able to get someone to chase those ships and capture them before the bloom on the flowering fidelia died.

# 6

"THEY OFFERED ME THE FLOWER AT TWENTY TIMES the price of my payments to you." Athenia stood in front of a wall with clear panels showing the blackness of space. She was a large woman with flowing silver hair. She wore a matching silver gown and silver rings on every finger. Silver dots outlined her eyes, accenting her dark skin.

Yu felt lost. He stood on a platform seven steps down from her. He could just barely see his own reflection in the clear panels. His eyes seemed larger than usual, his lips caught in a grimace. An illusion of the light made his curly black hair seemed streaked with gray. He looked older than he had just a few hours before.

Maybe he was older. Decades older.

He had lost the fidelia, and he knew it. The leader of the Black Fleet had tapped into his equipment and opened the ship's locks from the inside. Only one person had come on board, imprisoning him in his room, re-programming the ship's computer, and taking the fidelia.

"Did you take the offer?" he asked Athenia.

"The idiots didn't know the flower could die if mishandled. They had no idea that there is a time limit on the bloom. They want payment up front, and they're too far from here to meet within the seven-day window." Athenia stopped pacing, her skirts swirling around her. "So, no, I didn't pay them. And I'm not going to pay you."

He had known that was coming. "I'm sorry. I had no idea they were monitoring my transmissions. It seems that they knew what I was searching for."

"They knew what *I* was searching for," Athenia said. "The moment you contacted me, they were alerted. They had plenty of time to plan their little heist."

"I can go after them. I can find them—"

"And we still miss the window," Athenia said.

Yu's palms were sweating. He resisted the urge to wipe them on his pants. "There may be more flowering fidelias in that swamp. If I found one, I can find others."

She crossed her arms and looked down at him. "You forget our agreement. You had one fidelia. You lost it. You will not work for me again. Nor will you work for any friend or acquaintance of mine. I've already sent word through the various networks that you are inept. You should have planned for something like this."

*You should have warned me that the Black Fleet knew you were after the fidelia,* he thought, but didn't say. Instead, he said, "I'm trying to make this right."

"No, you're not. Had you done that, we wouldn't be in this situation. Now I'm out three years and more money than I care to think about."

"You haven't paid me any fees," he said.

"For which I am grateful. But you will repay your expenses."

He felt cold. He couldn't afford that. "Our agreement stipulates that I get to keep those expenses."

"Provided you made a valid search for the fidelia. I have no evidence of such a search."

"I found a flowering fidelia," he said. "I notified you of that."

"I have no proof that such notification is accurate. For all I know, you were trying to justify those inflated bills you sent me every quarter."

"I didn't inflate the bills," he said. "And I didn't lie about the fidelia. I have holoimages of the plant. I can prove to you that I had it."

"But can you prove to me that you didn't already sell it to someone else? Maybe that's how the Black Fleet got it. They paid you double what I offered and are now offering it back to me at a much higher price."

A flush rose in his face. "I'm not that kind of man."

"No," she said. "You don't call yourself a thief. You call yourself a Recovery Man. You don't steal. You recover."

That flush was so deep he felt like he was burning up from the inside out. "That's right. I recover things. I'm a professional. All of my interactions are professional. I trained with botanists so I wouldn't hurt the fidelia when I recovered it. That's the sign of a professional. Another sign of a professional is that I make agreements and I keep to them. I work for other people, not for myself. I do not steal. I trust that the people I work for truly need personal items recovered."

"In other words, you're not the thief," she said. "I am."

*Yes. That's exactly it. You're the thief. I'm the one who works for you and asks no questions.*

"No," he said. "All I'm trying to say is that I work in good faith. I do the very best I can."

"And thieves don't? It seems to me that the Black Fleet was quite prepared and very professional. They certainly got the better of you."

*And you,* he thought. *Especially if it was your transmissions they were monitoring.*

"Let me set this right," he said. "I'll get you a new fidelia and I'll recover the one from the Black Fleet. Think of what you could learn from a flowering fidelia past its bloom and one in the middle of blooming."

She glared at him. "I needed the blooming fidelia. You could not get that for me, so you're fired. On your way out, you will receive an exact accounting of the amount you owe me. I want the money within six Earth months, or I will add straight financial theft to the bulletin I sent out about you. At that point, I also will press charges through the Earth Alliance. You will be a wanted man."

The second threat frightened him less than the financial one. He had been a wanted man off and on throughout the Alliance most of his career.

She must have sensed that her threats didn't impress him. "You will pay me. Or at the end of six months, I will hire Trackers to find you, confiscate everything you own, and turn you in to the Earth Alliance. Is that clear?"

Yu nodded. It was clear, and it was much more of a threat than she knew. If he cleared out all of his accounts, he would have enough to pay her back, but he would have nothing left. It had taken him a lifetime of work to compile that amount of money. The expenses had been fierce on this case, and he had paid them willingly because he never thought he would have to reimburse her.

But she had the upper hand. She could do all the things she threatened and more.

"Surely we can come to some kind of arrangement," he said, his voice sounding timid even to himself.

"We already have an arrangement," she said and left the room.

# 7

Six months was not enough time to make the money that it had taken him a lifetime to earn. He considered various options: he could find another flowering fidelia and sell it, like the Black Fleet was doing. He could track down the Black Fleet and exact some kind of revenge. Or he could hire himself out for the large jobs he had avoided until this one.

But it had taken him three years to find the first fidelia, and without Athenia's money, he might not be able to find another.

He could go after the Fleet. But he was one unarmed ship against at least a dozen. And what could he do when he got there? Call the debt by asking them to return the fidelia? They said he couldn't do that. And besides, by the time he found them, the bloom would probably be gone. He would gain nothing, except maybe the Fleet's enmity.

And that was if he could find them.

He settled for the remaining option—hiring himself out for big jobs—only to learn that no one would take him. Athenia had ruined his reputation in all the circles that counted.

So he did the only thing he could do.

He went to the Gyonnese.

Ostensibly, he went to have them repair his ship. He assumed the Black Fleet had done something—tapped in, ruined a section, figured out a weakness he didn't know—and he wanted the Gyonnese to fix it.

But his actual reason for approaching them was to see what kind of off-the-books work they could muster for him.

In the past, he had turned down their off-the-books jobs. Those jobs always skirted the edge of Alliance laws in ways that made even a Recovery Man nervous.

But he couldn't afford to be so picky now.

# 8

Yu understood the Gyonnese as well as a member of one species could understand the members of another. He had lived among them off and on for the past decade, not because he liked them (he really didn't) but because their engineering skills fascinated him.

It was almost as if they saw the universe differently, as if the way things worked was an additional dimension, one that humans couldn't quite grasp. That was why he bought a ship modified by the Gyonnese, and why he did his best to gain their trust.

New Gyonne City spread like tendrils across a flat plain. From close orbit, the city's tendrils were impossible to distinguish from the tributaries of the continent's only river.

New Gyonne City was the Gyonnese's first colony city, founded on a moon not too far from Gyonne itself. Yu preferred the city, mostly because a section had been designed after the Gyonnese joined the Earth Alliance. That section of the city had things that Yu considered necessities—chairs, tables, a variety of human-compatible food served in actual dishes.

As he landed, he sent out word that he was available for work. He had never done that before.

After he had gone through decontamination, customs and immigration, he emerged into the main section of the port to find a group of Gyonnese officials waiting for him.

The Gyonnese were slender creatures, as fluid as their city. They weren't much wider than his thigh, with long bodies and even longer heads.

This group included some of the city's leaders. Most humans wouldn't have recognized them, but Yu had worked hard at distinguishing the Gyonnese's features.

The Gyonnese had eyes, placed in roughly the same position as human eyes, but whiskers composed the rest of their face. The whiskers were tiny, and varied in color and length depending on age and gender. The Gyonnese rubbed their whiskers together to create the sounds that composed their speech. To be understood by most humans, the Gyonnese had to use an amplifier.

Yu didn't need one to understand them. He also knew that speaking in a normal human tone would hurt their ears (which were hidden somewhere in their mid-torso).

"Hadad Yu." The Gyonnese closest to him was the one who spoke. The Gyonnese often designated one of their number to communicate with humans.

Yu nodded toward the speaker in acknowledgement, but spoke to the entire group.

"You have broadcast that you are available for hire. Is this thing true?" When the Gyonnese spoke, it looked like the flesh beneath their eyes undulated. In reality, it was just their whiskers as they rubbed together.

This was the moment Yu could back out, and he probably should. To have so many high-ranking Gyonnese waiting for him did not bode well for the job they wanted to hire him for.

But this might be his only chance at work. And the Gyonnese paid well, even if they often asked for vaguely illegal things.

"Yes," Yu whispered. He made sure the sound was so faint that most humans would think he was whispering to himself. "I sent a message that I am available for large jobs."

"You have angered someone in the Alliance," said the speaker. The others bobbed—their version of nodding.

"I have," Yu whispered. "I had been warned that she was an unreasonable client. I spent three years on her job, but she would not let me finish. Instead, she is spreading lies about me."

"That you are unreliable," said the speaker.

Yu wished he knew their names. When he was speaking to humans, he tried to use names to put them at ease. But the Gyonnese did not use names.

Instead, they had honorifics, which were based on what stage of life the Gyonnese was in. Some were Elders, others were Apprentices, and there was a whole list of honorifics in between.

"She has said I am unreliable," Yu whispered. "But an unreliable man does not work on a job for three years without payment. You know me. I have always worked well for the Gyonnese."

"That is why we are here. We need to hire you."

He figured as much. Normally, he would suggest a private place to discuss the work, but the Gyonnese did not meet aliens in private. Carrying on the discussion in the port was the best they would do for him.

"Tell me the job," he whispered, "and I will tell you if I can help you."

"We will pay your debt to this liar," the speaker said as if Yu hadn't spoken. "And then we will pay five times your normal fee."

He felt cold. His normal fee for the Gyonnese was always ten times larger than the fee he charged human clients. This job had to be huge.

"And," the speaker said, apparently taking his silence for reluctance, "we will pay your personal expenses in advance. Any change in the cost will work to your advantage. If the expense amount is more, you will submit a final bill. If it is less, you will keep the difference."

The muscles in Yu's back were so tight that they ached. He had to turn this job down now, before he heard their proposal. Because he knew the Gyonnese. They understood that this job wasn't one he would want to do. They were trying to bribe him.

And it was working. He would be able to keep his private funds, pay off Athenia, and have money enough to return to the small work that he preferred.

"What's the job?" Yu was glad he was speaking in whispers. He wasn't sure his voice would be steady enough to ask the question.

"We need you to recover a Fifth," the speaker said.

It took him a moment to understand. They didn't mean a measurement. They meant a type of Gyonnese. The Gyonnese had great trouble having children. Most Gyonnese only had one child, which was called the Original. But at the larval stage, the Original Gyonnese divided into several other matching Gyonnese. Humans couldn't tell the others apart. Biologically, there didn't seem to be a difference. But the Gyonnese could tell. A Second, Third, Fourth or Fifth was, to the Gyonnese, an inferior creature, subject to greater rules and stricter living conditions than the Originals.

Yu knew enough about the culture to understand that the Gyonnese who faced him now were all Originals. He was stunned that they had even mentioned the existence of a Fifth to him.

"I'm sorry," he whispered—and he truly was. He would have loved the money. "But while I am familiar with your culture and respect it a great deal, I am not sure I could tell a Second from a Fifth."

He knew better than to say an Original from a Fifth, which was the actual truth.

The Gyonnese surrounding him raised their whiskers over their eyes. The gesture made a whispery clicking sound, which was their version of laughter.

"We do not send you after a Gyonnese Fifth," the speaker said when after the whiskers had returned to their usual position. "We send you after a human Fifth."

*Humans don't have Fifths,* he nearly said, and then he realized what the Gyonnese meant.

"You want me to go after a clone?" He spoke out loud.

The Gyonnese scuttled backwards. He had done the equivalent of shouting.

"I'm sorry," he whispered. "I did not mean to speak so loudly. But by law, clones are humans, not items to be recovered."

That wasn't entirely true. Within the Alliance, clones were considered human for some parts of the law—if one was killed, it would be considered a homicide—but in other parts, clones were just as insignificant as the Fifths of the Gyonnese. In many parts of the Alliance, clones had no economic legal standing. The original child received the inheritance and all the protections accorded to a child in a family. The law considered the cloned child as if it were an orphan.

As far as Yu was concerned, however, clones were humans. He did not recover humans.

"You'll need a Retrieval Artist to find this Fifth," he said. Retrieval Artists usually hunted for Disappeareds, people who went missing on purpose, usually to avoid prosecution or death by any one of fifty different alien cultures.

"We have contacted seven such highly recommended 'Artists,'" the speaker said, "before it became clear to us that none will take our money. They work for humans only."

Of course. Yu hadn't thought of that. Retrieval Artists worked against alien cultures, not with them.

"A Tracker then," Yu whispered. "Someone used to finding people. I find things."

"A Fifth is not a person as we understand it," the speaker said.

That statement was accurate as far as it went. "Person" as the Gyonnese used the word only counted the Original.

"Does this Fifth live within the Alliance?" Yu asked.

"Yes." The speaker scuttled toward him. He realized that the Gyonnese thought the question meant he would take the job.

He took one step back, which was the Gyonnese equivalent of putting up his hands. "The reason I ask is this. If I recover a human Fifth that lives within the Alliance, I am breaking human laws. The action would be called a kidnapping. I could go to prison for the rest of my life."

He wasn't sure they understood what a kidnapping was, but they did understand prison. The Gyonnese had something similar for their own people, which was, he had heard, degrees worse.

All of the Gyonnese turned away from him. They merged into a small circle. They were discussing something, but he couldn't hear because they had shut off their amplifiers.

His stomach ached. He hadn't eaten well since Athenia ruined his life, and now the stress of this encounter was making him both hungry and nauseous. He wanted this meeting to end. He couldn't help the Gyonnese, and he wasn't sure how long it would take to convince them of that fact.

After a few minutes, they separated. They formed around him in a semi-circle. The Gyonnese used circles as their primary meeting formation, and to include him inside one was a great honor.

"We understand kidnapping. We have studied much human law," the speaker said to him. "We did not realize that such an act would apply to a Fifth. Our apologies."

Yu felt his shoulders relax. He would be able to leave soon. "I accept your apologies."

"We have another proposition for you instead," the speaker said.

Yu had a hunch he wouldn't like this one either, but he couldn't very well leave the circle.

"What's that?"

"We need you to recover a human criminal."

He was so nervous he wanted to make a joke: would any human criminal do? But he said nothing. He waited.

"Her name is Rhonda Flint. She has murdered generations of Gyonnese. She has been found guilty in Alliance court, but she has not complied with the court's orders."

"She's Disappeared?" he asked.

"No," the Gyonnese said. "She must turn over her Original child. But she has not done so. That child has Disappeared or so we believe."

"And no Retrieval Artist will help with this either, I suppose," Yu said. "But I know for a fact that Trackers will."

"Trackers believe the child dead."

Despite himself, Yu was intrigued. "You don't?"

"We think the Original might indeed be dead. But Rhonda Flint lives with a child which we believe to be a Fifth. If the child is not a Fifth, we want that child. If the child is a Fifth, then Rhonda Flint is in violation of her court order. She has hidden the Original in such a way as to invalidate our legal rights. We want to take her to court, but the only way we can do that is to bring her ourselves."

"Trackers," Yu whispered. "They are your only hope."

"Trackers must be hired through a human government. None will cooperate with us. We have a human lawyer who claims that such refusals negate Alliance law, but as we said, we cannot bring the case without her. So bring her to us. The same terms as before."

"I don't understand," he whispered. He had never seen the Gyonnese so serious. "The court can compel her to come forward."

"The court believes circumstances have discharged her debt," the speaker said.

"For mass murder?" The shock almost made him raise his voice again, but at the last second he caught himself.

"That is the problem. The Alliance—the humans within the Alliance—do not believe that she has committed a true crime. That is the problem with this system all along." The speaker crossed his long arms over his torso. It was an attempt to mimic the human gesture, but every time Yu saw it, it looked like sausages wrapped around a stick.

"I still don't understand," Yu whispered.

"You humans allow what you call Disappearance Services for people like Rhonda Flint—"

"I thought she hadn't Disappeared," Yu whispered.

A nearby Gyonnese touched the speaker behind his back. The speaker's whiskers flailed slightly, making a sound that didn't reach the amplifier.

"She did not Disappear, because the court and her corporation protect her. But let me be clear. It is the same thing. You humans commit crimes, serious crimes, and they do not fit in your customs, so you allow those criminals to escape, to build new identities. It is causing rifts in the Earth Alliance, one that may lead to the exclusion of humans from the Alliance if the situation isn't remedied."

Yu's head hurt. This was much more complex than he was used to.

"Okay," he whispered. "By your standards, she's a criminal."

"By anyone's standards," the speaker said. "She has committed mass murder. She is not going to be punished. We are going to demand punishment."

"Or what?" Yu asked. "Cause an interstellar incident?"

"That is not your concern. Your concern is recovering this woman for us."

*It sounds like you never had her,* Yu almost said. But he knew better.

"I'm not licensed for human trafficking," he whispered. No one in the Alliance was.

"It is simply the recovery of an unwilling criminal," the speaker said.

"Which I'm not trained for either. I work with *things*. Hire a Tracker."

"This woman works for one of the largest corporations in the human universe. No human government is going to cross it."

Which, Yu realized, was the crux of the problem.

"We will double the fee we initially offered you," the speaker said.

The coldness grew worse. Clearly, he was their last hope.

"Show me what she did," he whispered, knowing he was already lost.

# 9

Rhonda Flint worked for one of the largest corporations in the known universe. Aleyd developed products all over the Alliance. Twenty years ago, the corporation had leased a lot of land on Gyonne, and had negotiated various deals with the Gyonnese to market the Gyonnese's farming techniques to poor regions of planets with difficult environments.

The Gyonnese had a terraforming technique that worked extremely well with unusual environments. Aleyd would market that in exchange for permission to lease Gyonnese land for its work on colonial products.

One of those products was a new fertilizer designed by Rhonda Flint. It was an aerial spray, which she tested near one of the Gyonnese's larval beds.

The spray was lethal to Gyonnese larvae. Sixty thousand Gyonnese larvae died. Had these larvae grown, they would have been Original Gyonnese. One hundred and twenty thousand families probably lost the ability to reproduce. The effect to the Gyonnese was devastating. It was as if an entire section of the planet had been wiped out.

For the first time in his life, Yu understood both sides of an argument. The Gyonnese larvae had already split. The genetic material had been preserved in a secondary larval bed. From a human perspective, the equivalent of a twin's fetus had been lost. While that was a tragedy, it wasn't like losing an existing child.

But to the Gyonnese, who considered anything divided from the Original to be inferior, entire families had been destroyed forever.

The Fifteenth Multicultural Tribunal had no Gyonnese sitting on that particular bench at that particular time. For the court, the incident was an intellectual exercise. While it understood the Gyonnese position, it did not show much compassion for what was, to the Gyonnese, the loss of sixty thousand children.

As her punishment, Rhonda Flint was to give up all her children—living and any born in the future—to the Gyonnese. But Rhonda Flint's daughter died in a horrible accident not long after the court's final ruling. If Flint had succeeded in cloning the child, the clones would not be considered children under the ruling or, indeed, under Gyonnese law.

But the Gyonnese were sophisticated. They understood that to humans, children—whether they were cloned or created naturally—were considered human. They knew that Rhonda Flint would consider the clone a true child. So they, rightly, believed she had circumvented the rule of law.

The Gyonnese had given Yu all this material and sent him to a diplomatic conference room to learn about it. He watched the spraying, saw the Gyonnese mourn their young, watched the end of the trial. He saw a visibly frightened human woman burst into tears when the verdict was called. Her lawyer had argued that she wasn't liable for her actions, that the corporation was.

While the Gyonnese had ended all of their contracts with Aleyd, they believed punishment needed a living face. And that face belonged to Rhonda Flint.

The court agreed.

It was convenient that Flint's daughter died shortly thereafter.

Yu was shaking when he finished with the materials. Not just because of what he had seen, but because he knew—on a visceral level—that the woman he saw sobbing on the holoimages before him was a mass murderer.

The Gyonnese adored their children. Because families could only have one—not by law, just a simple matter of biology—the Originals were so precious that they were kept from outsiders until they reached young adulthood. Even then the Gyonnese treated the young with an affection that touched him more than he wanted to admit.

If the Gyonnese were right, and this woman had her daughter—the original child—cloned, then she was skirting the law and the legal ruling. And that was wrong.

Of course no Tracker would take this case. Human governments wouldn't understand it.

And Retrieval Artists—at least the ones Yu had met—would think that the Gyonnese were overreacting.

After all, there were four other identical "children" per larva. Humans would believe that those children should be treated equally with the Original. But the truth of it was, those children were not equal to the Gyonnese.

And that was what mattered.

Before Yu hesitantly took the case for the money. Now he was going to bring back Rhonda Flint to face the courts again because it was the right thing to do.

Hadad Yu was normally not the kind of man who did the right thing.

He wasn't quite sure what to do with his strong visceral reaction to Rhonda Flint's crimes. Perhaps he had learned a kind of empathy for the Gyonnese that he hadn't realized. Or perhaps he needed a kind of hatred to go against his essential nature and recover a human instead of an item.

Whatever the cause, he was now on the case. He would remain that way until Rhonda Flint was in Gyonnese custody—something he would bring about with the same kind of precision he used toward finding missing items.

# 10

First, he used the Gyonnese's information as the basis for his own research. He quickly learned that Rhonda Flint had moved from Armstrong on the Moon to Valhalla Basin on Callisto, one of Jupiter's moons. Callisto was the home base for Aleyd, which had turned Valhalla Basin into a company town where everyone had a connection to the corporation, even the visitors.

Second, Yu made certain that the original daughter was truly dead. He looked at the police reports, studied the visuals. He soon learned that Rhonda Flint now called herself Rhonda Shindo. Flint had been her married name. She had followed an old-fashioned custom and taken on the identity of the man who had fathered that daughter, a man Rhonda Flint/Shindo eventually abandoned.

Finally, Yu hired an assistant, a man he'd worked with before. Janus Nafti was strong and compliant. He was a big man who shaved his head and wore tattoos as if they were disguises. He wasn't very smart, but he worked hard. Nafti didn't question, did as he was told, and rarely spoke unless spoken too.

Yu promised him double the usual fee, telling Nafti that the Gyonnese were paying him twice as much as usual.

The rest of the preparations were simple. Yu researched Aleyd, Valhalla Basin, and Flint/Shindo herself. He learned that she now had an on-site job. She was allowed no contacts with races other than humans, and she kept her name off most research, even projects she spearheaded.

She claimed, in one paper she had delivered at an Earth-based conference, that she had taken a less adventurous position so that she could be home after school every day to be with her daughter.

Which led Yu to the Aleyd recruitment information system. He put in a request for Valhalla Basin, claiming he had family, and learned exactly how the systems worked there.

The houses were owned by the corporation and given to the employees according to pay grade. He even found floor plans and rough smart house schematics. He learned when the schools started, when they let out for the day, and which schools catered to what level of income.

Income was a specious term, since much of Aleyd's payments for its Valhalla Basin employees came in services, from medical care to shopping bonuses, all of which varied by pay grade. Essentially, everything he wanted to know about the entire community was available on Aleyd's recruitment site, including how to get through the port at Valhalla Basin with a minimum of fuss.

All of that relieved him. Kidnapping a human—no matter what the law or the Gyonnese called it—would be the most difficult thing he had ever done. He was happy that finding her, and figuring out the best times to take her, was easier than he expected.

He hoped everything else would be as well.

# 11

GETTING INTO VALHALLA BASIN'S PORT REQUIRED very little cunning. He bought seventy-five pieces of high-end Earth-made real wood furniture and resold them to Aleyd Corporation. His arrival on Callisto, then, was just that of a businessman making a delivery. He claimed a crew complement of three—two men and one woman—and hoped that no one would check how many crew members he brought into Valhalla Basin because the only one traveling with him was Nafti.

They unloaded the furniture quickly. They had permission to stay for three days should they need it. Yu hoped they wouldn't need it.

He had memorized the map of Valhalla Basin, but nothing had prepared him for the real thing.

He had expected Valhalla Basin to resemble the Moon's largest city Armstrong, with its cobbled-together dome, built over time, and buildings of all different styles and shapes.

But Valhalla Basin was uniform. The buildings in the downtown area seemed to have been built at the same time by the same architect. The dome was also uniform—one arched vista dominated by Jupiter, which loomed over the city like a round attacking ship.

He didn't need public transport to get to the neighborhoods. When he landed, he received credits, courtesy of Aleyd, to spend in local hotels, restaurants, and stores. The credits let him rent a vehicle for the day.

He wasn't sure if he should call the vehicle a car: it was larger than any car he'd ever seen, with six wheels instead of the usual four. The driver sat in the center, and any passengers had their own section behind him.

He had chosen the vehicle because the sectioned areas could be shut off and the doors double-locked from the front—a child-protection feature, he was told, but which seemed more like a prison to him.

Everything about Valhalla Basin seemed geared toward families and business. The downtown, with its austere silver buildings that turned color when the dome itself did, had the no-nonsense image cultivated by most Earth-based corporations. But the neighborhoods had a regimented personality.

He drove himself, Nafti, and what little equipment he'd brought into the neighborhoods, leaving the vehicle's talking guidebook on. The talking guidebook was designed for prospective employees, so its patter was upbeat and positive.

Even without the talking guidebook, Yu could tell when he got to the upscale neighborhoods. The more upscale the neighborhood, the more housing color varied. The houses got larger as well.

The talking guidebook explained all of this, also mentioning the perks of the house computer systems, something Yu had studied in depth before he arrived.

He'd paid a colleague to hack into the systems of the company that designed all the household computers for Valhalla Basin. The colleague had downloaded all the specs for the various systems, with a step-by-step guide for diverting the security system, wiping the memory clean, and taking over the House system without alerting the authorities.

Yu had run through it all on a practice model. He had made no mistakes, and his colleague believed he was ready to handle an actual House system.

Yu hated field testing, but in this case, he had no choice. He had to disable Flint/Shindo's House computer before he did anything else.

He parked half a block away from the address he had obtained through Aleyd's corporate records. Rhonda Shindo and daughter lived in upper level professional housing. Shindo had opted for the best possible kitchen and a spa in the corner of the backyard instead of a bonus room. She used the spare bedroom as a home office and added the optional second bathroom.

Yu had reviewed those plans so many times that he felt he knew this house. He'd toured the holographic model, he'd opened all of the various security systems, he had slipped through the doors as if they were his own. He was ready.

He only hoped Rhonda Shindo wasn't.

He had planned his arrival for the middle of the day, when Rhonda Shindo would be at work and her daughter would be at school. He wanted to establish himself in the house before either of them arrived, shut down the House system, and use the element of surprise to get Rhonda Shindo out of there with the minimum of fuss.

He had to deliver her alive and undamaged to the Gyonnese. He also had to check to make sure that Shindo hadn't done a secondary bait and switch. There was the slight possibility that her so-called cloned daughter, named Talia, was the actual original daughter, Emmeline.

Before he left, he needed to check for the mandatory cloning number, which was usually tattooed on the back of the head.

The house had a side entrance, made invisible from the neighborhood houses by nooks and crannies in the design. Valhalla Basin residents were encouraged to use the front entrance, in full view of the neighbors and the street. Most residents did, but Shindo didn't.

She did a number of things that weren't typical for Valhalla Basin residents, including a refusal to upgrade her House computer to the best model possible.

Yu's hacker colleague had already given Yu the repair code for the House system that Shindo was using. All he had to do was touch it into the small security panel on the side door, and the door clicked open.

"Nice," Nafti whispered.

Yu whirled on him. Nafti had prepared himself for this job by tattooing his entire face and extending the whites of his eyes so that his blue irises looked like mere slits.

"I was just saying." Nafti shrugged.

"Nothing," Yu whispered. "You're saying nothing from now on."

Yu knew that wouldn't last, but it would cut down on the random chatter. He stepped inside the house. The side door opened into a kitchen that smelled faintly of real Earth coffee.

"We have not put in a request for service," the House said in a kind, matronly voice. "I shall notify the home-owner of your presence immediately."

"The homeowner requested our presence," Yu said. That claim would stall the House system while it verified his statement.

He went into the living room—sparsely decorated with the provided Aleyd furniture and a few personal items—and opened the House's control panel. One glance confirmed that Shindo had the system he expected her to have, with no upgrades and no internal modifications.

This was the system he had already disabled in his practices and he did the same here. He set up the system to shut down any human's internal links, so no one could contact the authorities from the inside. He left the House's overall system mostly intact—so that environment, cleaning, and general maintenance went on as usual—but he dismantled every aspect of the security systems except the ones that would trigger an automatic silent alarm.

Which meant that the exterior security barrier was still active. All he did there was disable the cameras closest to the side door.

He saw that feature as a protection for himself as well. If anyone unexpected—even a police officer—approached the front door, the House would comment on it and ask him if he wanted to take action. The part of the House system that notified anyone outside of the house of an approach had already been disabled by the homeowner, probably because it would be annoying to be interrupted at work every time a neighbor came by.

Even though the work was easy, his heart was pounding. He was used to quick jobs. When he was recovering things, all he would do was enter, shut down the security system, and recover the item. He would already know where the item was, what it looked like, and how hard it would be to carry.

"Okay, we're in," Nafti said from the kitchen. "Now what?"

"You let me work," Yu said. "Go to the bedroom and wait. The woman will be here soon."

But not that soon. Yu figured he had about three hours to prepare the scene. He wandered through the common area. He had to set up the repeating holographic message that the Gyonnese wanted to leave behind. The message explained Rhonda Shindo's crimes, in case the Valhalla Basin police did not know she was a convicted felon under Earth Alliance law.

The message would give Yu time to escape with his prisoner and get to the rendezvous point. Because even though the Valhalla Basin police department was on Aleyd's payroll, it had to enforce Earth Alliance laws. And Earth Alliance laws allowed for the capture—or in this case, recapture—of a convicted felon.

The thing that the holoimage did not mention was that, as far as the Earth Alliance was concerned, the conditions of Shindo's sentence had been met and there was no need to take her back into custody.

If the Valhalla Basin police force was like any other force, it would take them a while to access that information and even longer to act on it.

By then, Yu hoped to have already turned Shindo over to the Gyonnese.

The side door rattled, then banged open. Yu jumped, half expecting some kind of exclamation out of Nafti. But, for once, the big man said nothing. Maybe he hadn't heard.

"Mom?" A young girl's voice echoed through the silent kitchen.

Yu's heart pounded. He had hoped to avoid the girl entirely. She should have arrived home long after her mother had.

"Your mother has not returned from work as of yet," the House said.

Yu felt a half second of relief. The House hadn't revealed his presence.

"What's that smell?" the girl asked.

Nafti's cologne. Yu had gotten used to it, but it probably trailed behind him everywhere he went.

"It is a mixture of yicia leaves and synthesized scent enhancers, probably initially sold in a spray form," the House said. "I am unfamiliar with the brand name, but I could find it for you."

"No," the girl said with irritation.

Yu pressed himself against the wall. She walked past him into the nearest bedroom. She was as tall as he was, and rail-thin. She also had the blondest hair he had ever seen.

"Just tell me where the smell is coming from," the girl said.

"That information is not available to me," the House said.

"What?"

Yu headed toward the bedroom, hoping it wasn't the one Nafti was waiting in. He didn't want Nafti to get to the girl first.

"What do you mean it's not available to you?"

"Exactly that," the House said. "Certain things are no longer within my purview. If you would like the controls reset, you must contact the homeowner and have her use the established protocols."

"Homeowner?" the girl said. "What—?"

Her voice cut off suddenly. Then there was a large bang, followed by a female grunt. Apparently Nafti had been waiting in that room after all.

Yu hurried in. Nafti had his strong arms wrapped around the girl. Her eyes were a pale blue and they flashed with anger.

"Who the hell are you?" the girl shouted. Then she said, "House! House! Notify security! Call the police! Call Mom!"

"I'm sorry," the House said. "My emergency system has been dismantled. If you would like to reinstate the programming, you need to…"

The House system continued speaking, but the girl screamed over it. She kicked at Nafti but he held her tighter, cutting her scream in mid-thrum.

"You're not supposed to damage her, remember?" Yu said. He had made that rule when he hired Nafti. Yu didn't want anyone to get hurt on this trip, particularly the girl and her mother. Not to mention the fact that the Gyonnese wanted Rhonda Shindo to be undamaged.

Nafti let the girl go. She staggered forward, gasping for air.

"Grab her arms and hold her, but don't hurt her," Yu said. "I have to check something.

Nafti reached for the girl and she slapped at him. The movement was ineffectual. She was still gasping for air.

Nafti caught the girl by the arms and pulled them behind her. Tears sprang into her eyes.

"Not so tight," Yu said.

Nafti loosened his grip. Yu walked up to both of them. The girl stared at him in complete hatred.

"Sit her down," Yu said.

Nafti sat. The girl had no choice but to do the same.

Yu crouched beside them. The girl continued to watch him, her pale eyes defiant.

"Bend your head forward," Yu said.

She raised her chin ever so slightly. She never took her gaze off him. He both admired her spirit and worried about it. If the Gyonnese had sent someone else, her attitude could have gotten her injured or worse.

"Bend your head forward," he said in his most menacing tone, "or we'll do it for you."

"No," she said. "And you can't make me."

The answer was childish. He hadn't expected it from her. She continued to watch him, her cheeks turning a pale rose—whether from fear or anger, he couldn't tell.

Yu sighed, and nodded to Nafti. Nafti clutched her arms with one beefy hand and put the other on top of her head, pressing it forward.

Yu brushed Nafti's fingers, releasing a little of the pressure. Then Yu pushed aside the hair at the base of the girl's neck.

He didn't see a cloning mark. By Earth Alliance law, clones were supposed to be marked with their number— the first clone getting a 1 and so on. He had expected to find a five.

That he found nothing made him nervous.

So had her behavior. Maybe he just wasn't used to sixteen year olds, but he didn't remember them being quite as reckless and childish as this girl. Maybe the Gyonnese had gotten it wrong. Maybe she wasn't the original child or a clone.

Maybe she was a sibling.

"How old are you?" he asked.

"How old are you?" she snapped back.

Nafti grinned at him. Yu glared. He didn't want the girl to know that she was impressing them.

"Cooperate, child," he said. "Then we won't have to hurt you."

She didn't say anything.

Nafti clutched the top of her skull and slowly turned her head until the strain showed in her neck muscles. Yu shook his head at Nafti but didn't verbally remind him to leave the girl alone.

Yu moved so that he could see the girl's face. It was red. Tears stained the corners of her eyes.

He wanted to tell Nafti to stop, but before he did, he needed to get control of this girl. So Yu said,

"It doesn't matter to us what condition you're in, so long as you're alive. Doctors can repair almost any injury these days, so long as you don't die first. But they can't take away the pain you'll experience until the injury is fixed. You'll always have the memory of that. We can guarantee it."

She blinked at him.

"Now," he added, "tell me how old you are."

"I'm thirteen," she said, tears in her voice.

He was trembling. If she were a sibling, he had to take her and the mother. He wasn't prepared for that. He'd only said that the ship had a crew complement of three. He'd have to find a way to explain the girl's presence.

"Thirteen?" he said. "Stop lying."

"I'm not lying." The tears made her voice thicker. "Honest I'm not."

"You can't be thirteen," he said.

"I am." Her hands clenched against the floor, but she no longer tried to get away. "You've got the wrong family."

He felt a thread of panic. The houses did all look the same.

"You're Rhonda Shindo's daughter, right?"

"Yes," she said. "But you confused my mother with someone else."

He didn't answer that. She had no idea who her mother was.

Nafti kept his hand on the girl's head, but he watched Yu. "Maybe the mother shaved 29 Earth months off her age."

Yu thought about that for a moment. Maybe the mother lied to the daughter. She had lied about everything else.

"Or maybe they're counting her age in units other than Earth time." Yu turned to the girl. "Tell me your age in Earth years."

A tear ran down her cheek. She looked confused. "I'm thirteen Earth years."

Yu cursed.

"The tag has to be on the back of the neck," Nafti said.

"Only in the Alliance," Yu said. What if Shindo had cloned the daughter outside of the Alliance? Then he wouldn't be able to tell if she was a clone or not.

"What tag?" the girl asked. "What's a tag?"

Yu ignored her. He reached for his pouch and said to Nafti, "A couple places do put the tag under the skin."

He opened the pouch and brought a penshaped laser identifier. He hated these things. They weren't always accurate. But it should at least reveal if she had a hidden tag.

She was watching him. "You're not going to cut me open, are you?"

The identifier couldn't cut open skin. It was designed so that it wouldn't harm anyone. But apparently, she didn't know that. So he decided to use it to his advantage.

"Naw, honey," he said coldly. "Head wounds bleed."

He moved the identifier toward her. She closed her eyes.

Nafti turned her head back to a normal position and Yu held the identifier about the base of the skull.

"Nothing," he said in frustration. He didn't want to take her with him.

"Some of these places allow tags anywhere on the back of the head, so long as they're not in front of the ears for humans." Nafti said. Yu wondered how he knew this.

Yu moved the identifier. He shoved more hair aside and then moved the delicate edge of her right ear. A number flared up at him.

"There it is!" Nafti said as if he had discovered it himself.

But Yu wasn't excited. He was irritated. The Gyonnese had it wrong. She wasn't a Fifth.

"It's a six," he said. "A damn six. When were you born?"

The girl was shaking. She gave the date and the year in Earth time, then repeated it in Alliance Standard.

"Thirteen Earth years ago," Nafti said as if Yu couldn't do the math himself.

"Six. That bitch put her here as a decoy." How many children had that woman created for the sake of her own ego? How many had been captured by the Gyonnese before being let go as unworthy?

"What?" the girl asked.

She had the right to know what her so-called mother did to her. She had to know that she wasn't here as a beloved child, but as an extra round of protection for her mother.

"You weren't born, you know," Yu said. "You were hatched. You know that, right?"

"What?" she asked again, her voice even smaller.

"Maybe she doesn't know," Nafti said. Was the girl getting to him too? "Or maybe she had things erased. You want to check?"

For once, Nafti had outthought him. Of course he would want to check. If the girl knew where the original was, then Yu could go back to the Gyonnese with that information—and without Rhonda Shindo.

"Please don't mess with my brain," the girl said. She sounded truly terrified for the first time.

Yu ignored it. He had to.

"I don't have the skill to do a full memory recovery," he said. He didn't have the skill to do a memory recovery at all. "I was just supposed to bring her back. Humans are out of my league."

"There are truth drugs," Nafti said. "I've used them before. Here, hold her."

And then he swung the girl toward Yu. Yu grabbed her, feeling startled. Nafti must have worked with Trackers. Otherwise he would have had no need for truth drugs.

Nafti got up and left the room. Yu's heart was pounding. Would truth drugs hurt the girl? He had no idea.

The girl didn't say anything. She just trembled. He respected that silence. She was terrified, but she wasn't going to beg.

Nafti returned with a small vial. He poured some leaves from it into his hand. Then he grabbed the girl by the face, forced her mouth open, and shoved the leaves into it, massaging her throat until she swallowed.

She coughed, and then choked. That was enough. Yu didn't care what she knew. He reached around and pulled the herbs out of her mouth.

Her eyes were already lolling in the back of her head.

"How much did you give her?" Yu asked.

"Normal dose," Nafti said.

"For what size human?" Yu snapped. The girl fell limply against him.

"I dunno. Most."

"This girl is younger than most. Get some water."

Nafti disappeared again. When he came back he had a glass. Yu rinsed the girl's mouth. He'd hate it if she died.

"Can this stuff kill?"

Nafti shrugged.

Yu glared at him. "House," Yu said. "Do you have medical protocols?"

"I do," the House said.

"And a baseline for the daughter of Rhonda Shindo?"

"I do," the House said.

"Analyze this and tell me if it will harm the girl." Yu looked at Nafti. "Go pour that truth drug on the card near the main control panel. *Now*."

Nafti disappeared into the living room. There was a momentary silence, and then the House said, "There are no harmful herbs here. Depending on the dose, the girl will either be quite talkative or she will sleep for several hours."

"Looks like we got sleep," Yu said to Nafti.

"If you would like," the House said, "I will do a body analysis to see if the herbs have interacted with anything in her system."

"Yes," Yu said. "Do that."

A small needle formed out of a nearby piece of rug. It took some skin and blood samples from the girl, and then disappeared into the rug again.

Yu stared at it. He knew there was a reason he didn't own his own home. It could attack him at any time.

"She will sleep for twelve Earth hours," the House said. "She has ingested no other drugs. She will awaken slowly and might be confused about what has occurred."

But he wasn't sure he would be off-planet within twelve hours. He had to make sure she didn't notify the authorities.

"Put her in that closet," Yu said to Nafti. "Make her comfortable. I'll take care of the rest."

## 12

THE REST WAS REPROGRAMMING THE HOUSE computer yet again. He locked the girl in the closet for twenty-four hours, making sure the House wouldn't let her out. He programmed the House computer to reset its security protocols in thirty hours, so that the girl could call for help if she couldn't figure out how to leave on her own.

That was the best he could do for her.

Then he prepared his message for the authorities.

He attached a holo unit to the side door. The unit replayed a recording of the spraying that Shindo had done. The Gyonnese had designed the holo unit. The Gyonnese had kept cameras on the field where their larvae were growing. The cameras were for the parents, so that they could see each moment of their child's development.

The recording had been edited down to just a few short minutes. First, it showed a wind-swept field under a blue sky. Light seemed thin, washing out the tall grass and the mountains beyond.

A running clock in both alien characters and regular numbers showed time lapsing. A vehicle hovered low over the grass, spraying a liquid.

Then the flying car disappeared and the grass died. The ground was brownish red, but parts of it turned black. The Gyonnese showed up, their whiskers moving in agitation. They bent in half and dug at the dirt, pulling up the dead larvae.

Larvae were usually light brown. These were black and shriveled.

The Gyonnese folded themselves in half, hands raised to the sky in a sign of complete and utter distress.

Eventually the image faded and words covered the screen: *Ten thousand died in the first wave. Twenty thousand families lost generations of genetic heritage. This act was repeated twice more. Sixty thousand Gyonnese have paid with their futures.*

*How has Rhonda Flint paid?*

The Gyonnese had set up a contact button at the corner of the image, and that proved the hardest to attach. Because the House's communications with the rest of Valhalla Basin had been shut off, Yu couldn't test to make sure he had set up the contact button correctly.

He had to hope that the instructions the Gyonnese had given him were correct.

He finished with very little time to spare. He checked on the girl—she was still unconscious, and she seemed unharmed. He made sure the closet was secured, then he went searching for Nafti.

Yu found Nafti watching a holoshow in the other bedroom. He had sprawled on the bed as if the place belonged to him.

Yu flicked the show off. "You were supposed to be monitoring the House."

"The House monitors the House." Nafti stood like a kid who'd been caught in his parent's room.

"And we shut that off, remember?"

"Oh, yeah."

Yu had to remind himself that he had hired Nafti for his muscles, not his brains. "We're going to wait for the woman outside."

"Wouldn't it be easier to catch her in here?"

It would have been, if Yu hadn't already shut down a lot of the House's systems and installed the holoimages in the kitchen. Rhonda Shindo would know the moment she walked in the house that something was wrong.

"Stop asking questions. Just do what you're told."

Nafti must have caught the note of exasperation in Yu's voice because he nodded. They collected everything they had brought, then Yu stopped and directed a house-bot to thoroughly clean every room except the kitchen and the closet part of the girl's bedroom. It wouldn't prevent the authorities from figuring out who took the woman — especially since the girl had seen him — but it would slow them down, and give them time enough to authenticate the message the Gyonnese had left.

That message would turn the attention from him to the Gyonnese. Then he could continue with his quiet life, finding little objects for people who paid him too much money.

He helped Nafti out of the house, found the man a hiding spot near the backyard—one that would be in the line of site from Yu's hiding spot—and instructed Nafti to move only when he got the signal.

Then Yu slipped into his own hiding spot, not too far from the side door.

Rhonda Shindo arrived five minutes later. She was slim like her daughter, but not as tall. She had the same bronze skin, but her hair was dark and pulled back. Her eyes were dark too. The girl had apparently gotten her striking looks from the father who believed her dead.

Shindo wore a pantsuit and heels, conservative like the rest of this place. She carried a briefcase, which surprised Yu. So far, she didn't seem to notice anything wrong.

He wanted her to just get inside the door before he grabbed her. Then he and Nafti could drag her to the backyard and their vehicle without catching much attention.

But she touched the door before opening it and drew her hand back, as if she had been shocked.

He could hear her speak—and the House answer—but the words weren't clear. He cursed silently. He hadn't expected her to talk to the House from the outside.

He crept forward. The House was reciting an ad for an upgrade and Shindo was looking annoyed.

She set down her briefcase as she said, "Just tell me if Talia put the electronics on the door."

"Not this time," House said. "The electronics were placed by a man who deleted his identity from my files. He conducted a thorough scrub but forgot to delete the section in which I monitored his deletion."

Yu silently cursed. What else had he forgotten? Or just plain missed? Could the House still notify security? Had it?

"Would you like me to bring that up on the wall panel to your left?" the House asked Shindo.

She was frowning, deepening the lines around her nose and mouth. "Yes, I would like to see that."

The visual would alert her to the problem. The element of surprise was slipping away from him, and he wasn't in the right place to alert Nafti.

So Yu stepped forward. He stopped right beside her. She was his height and thinner. He could probably subdue her himself.

"There's no need to see it," Yu said. "I did it."

She turned. Her eyes widened ever so slightly, the only sign that she was startled. "I don't think we've met, Mr.—?"

Politeness. He hadn't expected that. He waved his hand beside him, a small signal for Nafti, but he wasn't sure if Nafti could see it from this angle.

"We haven't met, ma'am," Yu said. He could be as polite as anyone else—more polite, even, if he needed to be. "But I know who you are. You're Rhonda Shindo. And just so that we remain on an even footing, let me tell you that I'm a Recovery Man."

Her body stiffened. "I've never heard of a Recovery Man."

"I think it's pretty self-explanatory." He was watching her, but out of the corner of his eye, he was hoping to see Nafti. "I recover things. Sometimes I even recover people."

That last was a lie, at least until today.

He added, "I work for the Gyonnese."

Her mouth opened. He couldn't tell if she was surprised or not.

"And don't play dumb about the Gyonnese," he said. "It's all on record."

That seemed to help her find her voice. She raised her chin, just like her daughter had done. It seemed to be the family gesture of defiance.

"That was settled," she said, "long ago, under Earth Alliance law."

She glanced toward the front of the house. She was thinking of running. If she got too far out, she would be able to call for help through her links.

"Actually," Yu said, staying close to her, "the case would be settled if you'd handed over your daughter to the Gyonnese. But you didn't. You hid her."

His words startled him more than they startled her. He wasn't talking to her just because he was waiting for Nafti. Yu still wasn't sure he wanted to do this.

He wanted to hear how she answered.

"No," Shindo said. "I didn't hide my daughter. Talia's been with me the whole time."

Nafti took that moment to show up. He approached silently, stopping half a meter behind her.

"Talia's not the child the Gyonnese want and you know it. Talia is too young." Yu took one step toward her.

Shindo took a step back and ran into Nafti. He didn't touch her—apparently remembering Yu's instructions this time.

She glanced over her shoulder and had to look up at Nafti's tattooed face. She looked from Nafti to Yu, and then toward the front again. She was trying to figure out a way out of this.

"Talia is the only child I have," she said.

Her answers weren't helping. She actually sounded panicked for the girl.

"Technically, she is the only child you have," Yu said, "but she's also what the Gyonnese call a false child. Very clever of you to have the number placed inside the skin, behind an ear. The tag itself intrigued me. The number we found was six. There are five others out there."

She looked trapped for the first time. Trapped and terrified.

"What do you want?" she asked.

"Tell me where the real child is." If she did that, he could leave without her or the girl. The Gyonnese wouldn't complain so long as they got the original child.

"Talia is my real child," Shindo said, and it sounded like she believed it.

Which disappointed Yu. Maybe she had killed the others, so that the remaining clone would be the only child. Or maybe she had just killed the original. Sometimes it took several attempts to get a viable clone. Five attempts wasn't unheard of.

"Technically," Yu said, "Talia's yours. But the Gyonnese want the original. The true child. Remember? I'm sure you do. It's the heart of the case against you."

"Please," she said. "Leave us alone."

She glanced toward the street.

"You know I can't do that," Yu said.

"I don't know that." Now she did sound panicked. "I've already told you where my child is."

"Give us the true child," Yu said, "or we take you."

Her mouth opened, and the panic became even more visible. She clearly hadn't thought anyone would take her. The courts only ruled on the children, as a punishment to her.

"You can't take me." Her voice shook. "I'm not on the warrant."

"We are under orders to take you." Yu was staring at her in contempt. She hadn't created those clones to have a child. She had created them as a buffer, to keep herself away from the Gyonnese.

Children, be they human or Gyonnese, didn't matter to her.

She raised that damn chin even higher. "Show me the legal document giving you that right, and I'll come freely, so long as you let me contact my attorney."

Nafti was watching all of this in confusion. He held his arms out slightly so he could grab her if he needed to.

"We don't need a legal document." Yu was going to take her. He knew that now. And he didn't care what the Gyonnese did to her.

At least the child would be all right. In fact, the child would be better off without her.

Shindo's chin came down. Her eyes were wild. She had finally realized that Yu meant to take her, no matter what.

"You need a warrant," she said. "The Gyonnese are part of the Alliance. They have to go by Alliance law, just like the rest of us."

Stupid, arrogant woman. As if she cared about the law.

"If you went by Alliance law," Yu said, "you would have given up the true child fourteen years ago. Humans flaunt this law all the time, with their Disappearance Companies that aren't prosecuted for secreting criminals away and giving them new identities. The Gyonnese decided if you people can do that, they can hire a Recovery Man."

Shindo lunged toward the front of the house. Nafti didn't even have to run after her. Instead, he just wrapped his arms around her, imprisoning her against him.

His grip was so tight that tears came to her eyes.

"You're coming with us," Yu said.

"Let me contact my lawyer." She didn't struggle like her daughter. She must have realized how futile struggling would be.

"If you had one, you'd've sent a message through your links by now." Although Yu knew better. He'd blocked link access this close to the house. "And he can't help you anyway."

"Kidnapping is a capital offense in human societies."

Yu shrugged. "We're just taking you for questioning."

"Against my will." Her voice rose in panic.

Nafti inclined his head toward the back, silently asking if Yu wanted him to drag the woman away.

"What did you do to Talia?" Shindo finally asked. It had taken her long enough.

"Nothing," Yu said.

"But you said—"

"I said we found the tag."

"How?" Shindo's voice broke. Now she was going to pretend that the daughter mattered to her. Although it was much too late to convince Yu.

"Just a little touch behind her head," Yu said. "She'll wake up soon enough. Then she'll miss you and go to the authorities and someone will find our message attached to your door, and they'll know that you're a mass murderer, who has so far managed to escape justice."

Her face was flushed. "Gyonnese law supercedes here. That's Alliance precedent, and under Gyonnese law—"

"The Gyonnese have true laws and false laws," Yu said. It was one of the many quirks of their civilization. He'd had trouble with that from the moment he started working with them. "They seem to thrive on more than one system. And while they prefer the known universe to see their true laws, sometimes they have to rely on the false laws."

"Like now," Nafti said into her hair.

"But Talia," Shindo said.

"You don't need to worry about her anymore," Yu said, as if she had ever truly worried about the girl. "Now it's time to start worrying about yourself."

# 13

"I'M NOT GOING TO BE ABLE TO LISTEN TO THIS anymore," Nafti said. "I have a headache."

He'd been saying that since they got back to the ship. They had imprisoned Shindo in a cargo bay and she'd been pounding on the door ever since. Even though the ship was large, the sound echoed throughout, thrumming into the bridge like the baseline of a particularly bad song.

"I mean it," Nafti said. He rubbed his bald head for emphasis. He had cleaned the tattoos off his face and removed the whitener from his eyes. Now his skin was dark and pristine and his eyes a deep, royal blue. "I'm getting sick here."

So was Yu. His head ached as well, but he wasn't sure if it was from the woman pounding below or Nafti's re-action to it.

"All right," Yu said. "Go down there and make her shut up."

"Do I hurt her?" Nafti had been frustrated ever since they got back from Shindo's house. Every time he'd come close to hurting her, Yu had stopped him.

"No," Yu said. "Just bargain with her. Or tie her up. Or something."

He didn't care as long as it got done. He had more important things to think about.

Like getting off this rock. It hadn't been hard to get Shindo to the ship. In fact, it had been surprisingly easy. No one questioned the way they hauled her to the vehicle, hauled her out of the vehicle, and dragged her through the port.

He supposed they figured if she really needed help, she'd send a message through her links. But he was using a small handheld that blocked any link communications. The device had limited range—it literally had to be on the person it was blocking—so no one else's links were affected.

To passersby, she looked drunk or crazy or both.

Valhalla Basin's port had its own departure customs, and they were almost as annoying as Bosak City's. Yu monitored the equipment, and finally the promised holoimage appeared in the center of the bridge floor.

The image showed his cargo ship in yellow, the ship ahead of his in green, and all the ships behind in red.

Yu had to acknowledge the notification. He brushed his hand across the top of the board, then got a timeline in response.

Not long until liftoff.

Then, in the little holoimage, the top of the port swiveled, and an opening appeared above his ship. His board confirmed: the first stage to liftoff had occurred.

His stomach turned. The moment he left Valhalla Basin with Shindo, he would have committed a major crime within the Alliance.

He had his defense ready—he had holoimages of the Gyonnese confirming the work as well as their promise that they were acting under the advice of their own legal counsel.

He was going to argue—if he had to—that what he had done was no different than a Tracker recovering a Disappeared.

Even though he had a hunch the Earth Alliance would see this differently. It certainly felt different. He kept thinking about that poor girl, stuffed in the closet, and wishing he had set the controls to free her sooner than twenty-four hours from the moment he left.

"Hey, Hadad?"

Yu jumped. He'd never heard any voice on the ship's speakers before except the voice of the ship herself. But this voice belonged to Nafti, and he sounded hesitant.

"What?" Yu made sure he sounded as annoyed as he felt.

"Um, this woman down here, she says the cargo hold is poisoned."

Yu punched a button to the left of the no-touch board. Nafti's ugly bald head appeared next to the image of the ships awaiting liftoff.

"I'm busy here," Yu snapped. "Why are you bothering me?"

"Because she listed at least five of the cargos that we carried in the last six months." Nafti looked scared.

"So? She found a manifest."

"You said we don't keep a manifest."

They didn't. Yu frowned. "How would she know?"

"She says that there's contaminants in the hold."

"Nonsense," Yu said. "We have a service that cleans everything."

It wasn't really a service. It was a bunch of cleaner bots he'd liberated from a previous owner. They were supposed to glow red when they reached their limit of hazardous materials.

"Well, the service ain't working," Nafti said.

The timer was blinking. His ship on the holoimage in front of him had turned a pale lime as the yellow blended into the green.

"I don't have time for this," Yu said and deleted Nafti's image.

Then Yu ran his hand above the board, feeling how easily the ship rose upwards. Silent, maneuverable—empty.

His sensors told him that the port had indeed opened its roof for him, there were no shields, and he was clear to take off.

Which he did.

Then he flicked an edge of the board.

"Your wish?" The ship asked in its sexy voice.

His cheeks flushed. He needed to change the voice to something more appropriate. "Scan cargo hold five for contaminants harmful to humans. And I don't want the chemical names. I want the street names."

"Such a scan would be harmful to the life form inside the cargo hold."

"Then do a scan that won't hurt her," Yu snapped.

"I have a list of the contaminants," the ship said. "Some do not have street names. I am confused as to how you would like this information. Would you care for the chemical names in the absence of street names? Or would you like symptoms and cause of death?"

"Just scroll through it," he said.

The ship created its own holoscreen, and presented a list that scrolled so fast Yu had trouble reading it.

But what he did see chilled him.

He cursed. "Ship, how good are our medical facilities?"

"Adequate to most needs."

"How about someone exposed to all that crap you're scrolling at me?"

"Ah," the ship said as if it were human. "We have adequate equipment, but no guiding medical persona. I can download something from the nearest human settlement, but I can't guarantee its ability to solve any problems that might arise—"

"How soon before someone trapped in that cargo hold starts showing symptoms?"

"From which contaminant?" the ship asked.

"Any of them," Yu said, wishing the damn computer wasn't so literal.

"Well, the first compound—"

"No," he said. "When will the first symptom from anything in that hold show up?"

"Mr. Yu," the ship said in that rich voice, which at the moment seemed more sulky than sexy, "symptoms should have started appearing within the first hour of contamination."

"Scan the life form. Is it healthy?"

"I do not have a baseline for my scan. I do not know what condition the life form was in before it got on the ship."

"Just scan her, would you?" He clenched a fist, then opened it slowly. He didn't dare hit a ship that ran on touch.

"The scans are inconclusive. If the life form was in perfect health, then it is showing symptoms," the ship said.

Yu cursed again. "How long do we have before the illnesses caused by this stuff become irreversible?"

"Impossible to say without a baseline," the ship said.

"Assume she was healthy," Yu snapped.

"Then two to twenty-four Earth hours. I would suggest a treatment facility, since you do not want to download a medical persona. Would you like a list of the nearest venues?"

Yu rolled his eyes. Any treatment facility in this sector of the solar system would be an Earth Alliance Base. He didn't dare go near those places.

"Download the best persona you can find," he said. "Better yet, download two or three of them. Pay the fees if you have to. I want cutting edge stuff. Modern technology. Nothing older than last year."

"Yes, sir," the ship said. "This will take fifteen Earth minutes for the various scans and downloads. May I suggest you remove the life form from the cargo hold and put it in quarantine?"

"You may suggest any damn thing you want," he muttered. But he opened his links, and sent a message to Nafti.

*Get her out of there, but don't go near her. Put her in the quarantine area, the regulation one for humans, okay?*

*How do I get her there without touching her?* Nafti asked.

*I dunno,* Yu sent. *Tell her she's going to die if she doesn't do what she's told.*

*But you said we can't kill her,* Nafti sent.

*Not us, stupid,* Yu sent. *The hold itself'll kill her. Tell her the quarantine room is our exam facility. She'll run for it.*

*Hope you're right,* Nafti sent, then signed off.

Yu hoped he was right too. Because this job was a lot more trouble than he had bargained for.

# 14

Yu monitored the decontamination from the bridge. He wanted to avoid the woman as much as possible—not because she was contaminated, but because he didn't want her face burned into his memory any more than it already was. He wanted to be done with this job—and quickly.

Unlike some of his equipment, the decontamination machine was state of the art. He needed the best for his own use. Often he went into areas that weren't Alliance supervised or Alliance approved. He didn't want to wear an environmental suit all the time, and he didn't want to bring back any exotic diseases.

Shindo's decontamination went well. The machine caught and eliminated more than 95% of the contaminants. The remaining 5% would be tough to get, however, and that was why he needed the medical personas.

He had them installed in the medical lab which he had never used. He kept the lab well stocked, however, since he traveled alone so often.

Nafti had supervised Shindo's trip from the cargo hold to the decontamination unit to the medical lab.

Then Nafti had locked her in there, and had gone exploring the rest of the ship himself.

Yu didn't know what Nafti was about, but he could guess. The man was a horrible hypochondriac, and he was probably trying to see if those contaminants had spread from the cargo holds to the rest of the ship.

A bell sounded. It was an audio alert that he had set up so that he would notice any unusual behavior.

"Yes?" he said to the ship.

"The medical lab has sealed itself off," the ship said.

"What does that mean?" Yu asked.

"I can no longer access information from the medical lab," the ship said.

"How is that possible?" Yu asked. But he knew. The ship had several systems grafted one on top of the other. If a knowledgeable person managed to tap one system, that person could lock out the remaining systems.

Apparently Shindo was more knowledgeable about ship's systems than he knew.

Yu cursed and bent over the board, trying to override whatever the hell she had done. He had investigated her as best he could before taking this job. He had thought he knew the limits of her knowledge.

She was a scientist, but one that specialized in chemical and biological systems. She had never flown a ship, never taken piloting classes, never so much as hired a private vehicle.

She seemed to have no technical skills at all except for the ones needed for her job.

Apparently she had more technical skills than he realized.

The door to the bridge opened and Nafti came in, wearing a battered environmental suit.

"You were wrong to trust those bots," Nafti was saying. He tapped on his suit. "You should be wearing one of these. You should go through the decontamination just like that woman did."

Yu didn't say anything. He had to concentrate on getting the medical lab back on line. Whatever the hell that woman was doing—good or bad—it worried him.

He was hoping it was just the new medical personas causing a glitch in the system, but if that was the case, so far he couldn't find it.

"You're not listening!" Nafti said.

Yu sighed. He hadn't been listening. But he lied. "I am listening. You don't understand."

"What don't I understand?"

"That you're a hypochondriac."

"What?"

"You got a headache when she started pounding. Then the canny woman mentions contaminants, which all ships have, and you go off the deep end. You put on that suit which, by the way, looks like it might have some integrity issues, and you go all over the ship looking for contamination, forgetting that the suit is probably contaminated from its contact with the hold."

Nafti looked down. The suit creaked as he did so, and Yu saw a rip along the neck.

"I did carry the wrong cargo in the hold," Yu said, "and I clearly didn't double-check whether or not the bots were full. I thought they worked. Obviously they didn't. But the ship is fine or we wouldn't have been allowed in and out of the ports, especially the ports in the Earth Alliance."

Which wasn't really true. He had dozens of ways to make sure his ship wasn't thoroughly inspected.

"Honestly?" Nafti sounded vulnerable.

"Yes, honestly," Yu said. "Remember that the holds have their own environmental systems. I showed you that when I hired you years ago. You asked about it."

Nafti reached up and removed the helmet. His face was covered with beads of sweat and his skin was red. Obviously the suit's environmental system hadn't worked properly either.

Yu tapped a few areas on the security monitor, trying to get access to the medical lab.

"I did ask, didn't I?" Nafti said.

"Yes," Yu said.

"I'm not a hypochondriac," Nafti said.

"Then what are you?"

"A worrier."

"What would you have done if this entire ship were contaminated and I refused to pay for your medical help?" Yu asked.

"It's not, right?" Nafti asked.

Yu ran his hand along the security board. "What did I just say?"

"You said it wasn't."

"Then maybe you should believe me," Yu said, "and stop thinking about the authorities."

"I wasn't," Nafti said.

"Deny that you would demand a full decontamination of the ship when we got to the next port," Yu said.

"It was only sensible if the ship's contaminated."

Yu leaned forward. "Think, you dumbass. What happens when you get a full decon?"

"The ship gets inspected…." Nafti's voice trailed off. "Oh."

"Yeah, oh. Do you know how many unapproved systems I have on this ship?"

"Is that why you've never had an inspection?"

"What do you think?" Yu snapped.

Nafti wiped at his face with his gloved hand. "Sorry."

"You should be," Yu said. "When I hired you, I demanded your full trust. You violated that today."

"I got scared."

"I know." Yu double-checked the security board a final time. "Take off the suit."

"I'm not sure I should."

"It's got a rip in the back. It never worked right. We've got to destroy the thing."

Nafti reached around back, then stuck a gloved finger inside the rip and started. Apparently, he had touched his own skin. He cursed.

"Next time, let me do the thinking, okay?" Yu said. "I didn't hire you to think."

Nafti unhooked the front of the suit. The fasteners still worked. They opened themselves quickly once he started the sequence.

"Sorry," Nafti said again.

He stepped out of the suit and left it in a pile near the navigation controls.

"I need you to get back to work," Yu said.

"Can I go to my quarters first? I'd like to change."

And he'd probably shower and linger, making sure he hadn't contracted anything from the flawed suit.

"No," Yu said. "Get to the medical lab."

"Why? They're diagnosing her. She should be there for a while."

"She should," Yu said, "and so far as I can tell, she still is."

"What do you mean so far as you can tell?"

"The lab isolated itself."

"What does that mean, isolated itself?"

"Maybe the three medical programs we just bought overloaded the system. That's what I hope it means."

"You think she could've done something."

"I doubt it," Yu lied.

Nafti squared his shoulders. He looked reluctant to leave.

"When you're there," Yu said, "you can have the medical system make sure you're healthy, okay?"

Nafti brightened. "Okay."

He kicked the suit aside and left the bridge.

Yu summoned one of the cleaning bots, and gave it orders to pick up the suit and send it through the ship's disintegration unit.

Then he tried the security monitor again. Nothing. He couldn't get through to the lab. He tried opening a back door and going at the lab from the basic part of the system. Still not possible.

He might have to dismantle the system from the outside just to get to her.

Yu sighed. That would be too much work.

If she wasn't out by the time they got to the rendezvous point, he would dismantle the system.

Otherwise, he would wait to see if Nafti could bully his way inside.

If anyone could do that, it would be his hypochondriac employee. Nafti was too scared to be denied access for long.

# 15

YU WAS BEGINNING TO PANIC.

The medical lab had been on its own for almost an hour which was long enough for someone with hacking abilities to find links to the ship's control panel.

Yu had realized that about ten minutes ago and set the panel to respond only to his vocal and touch commands, hoping he wasn't too late.

Damn that woman. She was smarter than he had thought.

And Nafti hadn't contacted him, which Yu had thought he would. The moment Nafti had gotten a diagnosis from the medical personas, he should have told Yu. He would have told Yu.

Which led Yu to believe that Nafti hadn't gotten into the lab yet.

Then the door to the bridge opened. Finally. He checked the controls and saw that the lab was still off-line.

"Took you long enough to get here," Yu said. "What's she doing down there?"

Something felt wrong. He couldn't quite say what it was—a faint scent, a sound—but whatever it was, it made him turn.

Just in time to avoid being jabbed with a hypo.

The woman was in front of him, her hair falling across her face, her skin covered with reddish blisters, her eyes wild. She dropped the hypo and grabbed something from her belt.

He reached for her.

She slashed at him, and he yelped. Pain burned through his palm.

She was holding a laser scalpel.

He cursed and backed away. A laser scalpel was a close-up weapon. His hand was useless. His fingers ached, and two of them wouldn't bend.

She'd severed something.

"What the hell are you doing?" he asked as he continued to back away. She came forward, the scalpel extended as if it were a knife.

"Saving myself," she said.

"Where's Nafti?"

"In the medical bay," she said. The tone of her voice was odd.

Yu's heart started to pound even harder. Nafti had confronted her, and he wasn't here. Had she attacked him too?

She lunged at Yu, and he moved to the right, grabbing her shirt with his left hand. More hypos fell onto the floor. She whirled, slashing with that vicious laser. It nicked his side—he felt the burn, knew it wasn't as deep as the cut to his right hand.

He had to do something, and quick.

He yanked her toward him with the shirt, let go, and for a brief moment, thought she'd regain her balance. She didn't. He grabbed her by the hair, and forced her head back.

He shoved his foot into her knees, forcing her down. She slashed, getting a thigh this time, and the wound brought tears to his eyes.

He felt a moment of surprise—she might actually win this fight—and then he smashed her face into the side of the console.

She went limp, but he didn't trust it, so he smashed her face again. Then once more just because she had pissed him off.

Stupid woman.

He let go of her hair and she toppled.

She didn't move.

He hadn't expected that. He stood above her for a moment, catching his breath, feeling the ache from his various wounds.

She had no training as a fighter. It would have shown up in her records.

But then she'd had no computer training either that he'd known of and look at what she had done in the medical lab.

The medical lab. Where she had gotten her weapons.

Then somehow she had snuck up here without letting the computer know where she was, and nearly took over the bridge.

Nearly took over his ship.

He was shaking. She could have killed him.

He collected the laser scalpel and its friends—she had hidden two more—as well as the hypos. He found cydoleen pills in her pocket and recognized them as extreme anti-toxins. He put those back. The medical personas had probably given them to her to help with the contamination.

Then he searched the rest of her, finding two more scalpels—one against her ankle and another between her breasts.

He set all the makeshift weapons aside, dragged her to a chair on the far side of the bridge and threw her in it. She listed to one side. She was covered in blood—and it looked like he had broken her nose.

"Computer, lock her into zero-g position in Chair Six."

The chair closed around her, so that she couldn't float. Zero-g position also kept her a prisoner, unable to move, unable to set herself free without the proper commands.

Still, he made sure. This woman was smarter than he had given her credit for.

"Release her on my command only."

The computer cheeped its affirmative.

Her head lolled forward, hair covering her face.

Yu studied her for an extra minute, stunned she had gotten so close.

Then he examined his wounds.

His thigh was cut open. She'd barely missed the artery. He would need some medical attention to close the wound properly, but that one wasn't life-threatening.

Neither was the wound on his side. He'd lost a chunk of skin, but nothing else. He didn't know enough about his own internal anatomy to know if she'd gotten close to anything important.

But his hand was an issue. He could see the bones and the connective tissue, some of it severed. The pain was exquisite.

Repairing that might take more than three cheap medical programs and some bandages. He'd probably have to stop at some space dock, and have a real expert repair his hand.

Or replace it.

He shuddered, then he kicked Chair Six. The woman's head lolled to the other side. Blood dripped from her nose. Yu'd done some damage of his own.

He was pleased about that. He'd leave her untreated. She could feel the pain for a while.

Behind him, the computer cooed. That was a different kind of alert, to let him know that whatever he'd been working on had succeeded.

In this case, he'd been trying to get into the medical lab. The computer had finally broken through whatever she had set up.

He turned to the nearest console, and saw images of the medical bay.

Nafti was crumpled on the diagnostic table, clearly dead. None of the medical avatars had appeared around him. So much for state-of-the-art. Somehow Nafti had been murdered in the very place that should have saved his life.

Dammit. Yu had liked Nafti, no matter how much of a worrier the man had been. The big dumb lug wouldn't complain any more. He'd been so worried about dying from a disease that he probably hadn't realized he was in more danger from the woman.

Nafti had underestimated her.

They both had.

And Nafti had paid for it with his life.

# 16

Yu limped to the medical lab. He thought about having the bots bring the medical supplies to him, but he wasn't sure it was a good idea. The medical lab had been off-line and he wasn't sure if Shindo had tampered with more than the security protocols.

Maybe she had damaged the bandages or the medicine. He wanted to see for himself.

And he had a hope—a tiny hope—that Nafti wasn't dead, just unconscious. Or maybe even imprisoned, the way that Yu had imprisoned Shindo. Maybe she had somehow rigged up the cameras so that the image Yu saw of Nafti's body was a false image.

Yu had left her on the bridge, imprisoned in the zero-g chair. He'd also put a security bubble around her, so that she couldn't wake up and start talking to the ship. No matter what she had rigged—if she had rigged anything—she wouldn't be able to access it from inside that bubble.

He was so light-headed by the time he reached the medical lab that he thought he was going to pass out. The lab's door stood open, and he could see Nafti, sprawled on the diagnostic table, just like he had been in the image.

Nafti's eyes were closed, but his skin was an unhealthy shade of whitish blue. The diagnostics were running on the screen behind the table, and all of them read flat.

Nafti was dead.

Still, Yu touched his hand ever so lightly. The skin was cooler than it should have been. Nafti had been dead for some time.

Yu stood over Nafti for a long moment. The man looked lonely in death. Lonely and terrified, even though the dead human face never held an expression.

Yu clenched a fist. Damn Shindo. Killing Nafti like that. Cold-bloodedly. No wonder she had been able to kill the Gyonnese larvae, if humans meant so little to her.

He touched Nafti's hand one final time. "Sorry," Yu whispered.

And he was. As irritating as Nafti could be, Yu didn't mean to get him killed.

Black spots appeared in front of Yu's vision. He was going to pass out soon if he didn't do something.

He scanned for a chair, and saw one not far from the diagnostic table.

The rest of the lab looked like it was ready for use. He'd been expecting a war zone. Instead, he saw medications lined up on a nearby table, laser scalpels and bandages sticking out of drawers and a drug list cycling on a screen nearby.

"I need assistance," Yu said as he slumped into the chairs.

A medical avatar appeared. It had the form of a woman. The avatar was carefully formed so that she wasn't too tall or too thin. She had light tan skin and eyes which were rounded with a touch of angle at the edges. Her hair was a neutral brown, her eyes also brown, and her features spaced in that precise way that computer programmers thought average. The avatar wore a white smock over her brown slacks, and fake compassion filled her fake eyes.

"What happened here?" she said.

"Drop the patter and treat me," he said.

She examined his wounds, picking at the edges of each carefully. After a moment, she said, "None of your wounds are life-threatening. But you need more than a medical avatar for that hand. I can bandage it up, but I cannot make it useful."

"I just need it functional enough to get me to the next base," he said, even though he wasn't going to the next base. He was going to drop off Shindo and get the hell out of the sector. Then he would deal with the hand.

"Understood," the avatar said.

She cleaned the hand and put some kind of disinfectant in it, shooting him up with all kinds of medicines that she explained as she worked.

Finally, he said, "I don't care what you're doing. Just don't tell me about it."

He didn't even want to watch her work. If she did it wrong, she did it wrong. The doctors on whatever base he stopped on could fix the mistakes the avatar made.

So Yu ordered up a visual of Nafti's last moments. The poor guy seemed to have had no trouble getting into the lab. Shindo had been staring at the laser scalpels, probably planning to use them as a weapon. She had turned when the door opened.

Nafti had looked like the patient, not her, despite the pustules forming on her face. He just looked frightened.

He said, *I thought we got medical programs.*

*You did,* she said. *I turned them off.*

*Why?* The word was plaintive.

*Because they have no more training than I do,* she said.

"Stop playback," Yu said. His stomach turned. That was how she had gotten Nafti onto the diagnostic tables. By pretending an expertise that she didn't have.

Or maybe she did have that expertise. She specialized in biology and chemistry after all.

Yu looked at his hand, now carefully bandaged. The medical avatar was working on his leg.

Shindo certainly seemed to have a lot of knowledge about where to damage him. He had been twisting away from her. If he had faced her, she might have sliced right through him.

She was dangerous, more dangerous than the Gyonnese had led him to believe. She had seen Nafti's weakness, exploited it to get him to trust her, and then she had killed him.

Big, dumb bastard.

"Hurry up," Yu said to the medical avatar.

He didn't dare leave Shindo alone too long.

## 17

HE MANAGED TO MAKE IT TO HIS CABIN, CLEAN up and change clothes long before Shindo opened her eyes. When he got back to the bridge, she was still unconscious. He took down the security bubble, made sure that the ship was still on course for the rendezvous, and then set about finding any modifications that Shindo had made to his ship's systems.

He had been working for an hour before she woke up.

"I could have suffocated." Shindo's voice was nasally and thick. Her broken nose was making it difficult for her to talk.

He turned away from the console and crossed his arms. The movement hurt, but he didn't let her see that. He didn't want her to know how badly she had injured him, although he figured she probably had a clue from the heal-it field bandages the avatar had placed on him.

"You didn't suffocate," he said.

Her face was black and blue, and so swollen that she barely looked human. But those eyes were the same. They flashed as they met his.

"You never leave an unconscious person with a broken nose untended," she said. "You don't know where the blood will go, what happens to the shattered bits of bone. You have no idea if that person is going to make it through the next few hours."

"Yet you did well enough to wake up and harangue me." He leaned against the console. "I monitored you. No sense delivering a dead criminal to the Gyonnese. Then you're not worth anything—to me or to them."

He had to work to keep his voice flat. In fact, he had to work at remaining near that console. He wanted to walk over to her and slap her across that bruised face.

"Don't worry," Yu said because she was just staring at him. "The rendezvous time is close. You'll be able to move then."

She licked her lips, but he couldn't tell if that was from nervousness or from the pain. "I'll pay you double what they're paying you to take me home again."

He smiled. So she was afraid. Terrified, not just of him but of the Gyonnese.

He liked the fact that she was terrified. It made him feel better.

"On the salary Aleyd pays you, you would pay me?" He shook his head. "It would take the rest of your life to pay my fee. Two lifetimes to double it."

"I would get the money from Aleyd," she said.

"Because they have an interest in keeping you out of Gyonnese hands?"

"Yes," she said.

So that was how she had gotten so far. Her corporation had backed her. They had probably provided the lawyers and maybe even the cloning service for her child. Had they killed the original child too? Or just Disappeared it?

No wonder the Gyonnese were angry. They knew that they had no chance of getting justice, even before the case began.

He walked toward her. He let his smile fade and the hatred he felt for her show in his eyes.

She squirmed in the chair, but she couldn't get free. She was breathing shallowly, a sign of growing fear.

"You killed my partner," he said.

"He wasn't your partner," she said. "He was your employee."

Interesting that she believed the distinction was important. Did she rank human lives the way she ranked humans above aliens?

If so, she would never understand why Nafti's death made Yu so angry.

So he said, "You tried to kill me."

She nodded, hitting her chin on the edge of the chair and wincing. "I felt like I had no choice."

Well, that excused everything. He was willing to die because she had no choice. He kept that sarcastic thought to himself, and made sure he kept his arms crossed despite the pain.

"And now do you feel like you had a choice?" he asked.

She licked her lips again. "I hadn't realized you were being paid."

She was lying. And even if she wasn't, he wasn't going to let her know that he thought her stupid.

"Why would I steal you otherwise?" he asked.

"I don't know," she said. "You could have been some kind of vigilante."

"Out to get mass murderers and bring them to my ship?" He permitted himself a small chuckle. "So I'm some kind of vigilante hero in your fevered imagination."

She winced. "I'm not a mass murderer."

"At least, not intentionally," he said, knowing the lie she would tell him. The Gyonnese believed the deaths were intentional, that she had been testing a weapon. He had no idea who was right.

The result was the same. The larvae were dead.

"Not intentionally killing someone makes it better right? Like feeling you had no choice in killing me. That mitigates it, doesn't it?" He couldn't keep the sarcasm out of his voice now.

Her wince grew into a frown. He wasn't sure if he was reaching her or just convincing her that she had no hope of getting away from him.

"Now you've killed a man with your bare hands," Yu said, unable to let it go. "How does that feel?"

She raised her chin. He had gotten to her.

"How does it feel beating a woman within an inch of her life?" she asked.

He smiled again. And this time, he meant it. "After she tried to kill me? Exhilarating."

She studied him for a moment. Then she bit her lower lip, as if she were thinking.

Finally, she said, "I can get Aleyd to pay you. We can set something up, some off-world account, and they can wire the money. They will do it. They paid for my defense—"

"And that didn't work, did it?" Yu said.

"—and they paid to relocate me. They want me to stay away from the Gyonnese. Not all the suits are settled."

He tilted his head back. She actually thought he would bargain with her. Did she think everyone as crass as she was?

"If Aleyd kills you," Yu said, "then the Gyonnese won't have you."

"If Aleyd wanted me dead," she said, "it would have happened long ago."

That was probably true. They wanted something else from her.

Or they felt she was too valuable an asset to lose.

"You're asking me to trust you," Yu said.

"No," Shindo said. "I'm trying to figure out the best way for you to make a profit."

She wasn't even a good liar. "And for you to survive."

"Of course," she said. Then coughed so hard that she spit blood on the travel chamber's exterior. "You injured me badly. You might want to get those fake medical idiots up here to set the nose."

"You injured me just as badly. I might lose my right hand."

Her expression didn't change. She didn't care. The woman had no empathy at all.

"They build better hands now than we're born with," she said. "Consider yourself lucky."

He clenched his good fist. "You're a cold bitch."

"And you're a coward," she said.

He blinked at her, startled.

"If you had any guts at all," she snapped, "you'd take my proposal."

"If I had any guts at all, I'd take your proposal and then sell you to the Gyonnese."

Her eyes opened wide. She clearly hadn't thought of that.

"Why do they want me so badly?" She was trying for plaintive. It wasn't working. "The case they had against me was settled."

"They think you broke the law."

"I did, according to the court," she said. "That's why I lost."

"After the case got settled. They think you hid your child from them."

"You saw Talia. I didn't hide anyone."

"The original child," he said.

"Is dead."

For the first time, he couldn't tell if she was lying. And he wasn't even sure he cared. She wouldn't tell him where the original child was, not even to save herself. That much was obvious.

But then, she also knew that he wouldn't kill her. So she had no reason to tell him.

She might tell the Gyonnese.

"The Gyonnese think the child is alive," he said. "They're going to use you as an example."

Her eyes seemed to get even wider. "An example of what?"

"They're trying to prosecute anyone who helps Disappeareds."

"But I'm not a Disappeared."

"Your child has Disappeared." He let his arms drop, then winced again as his right hand bumped his leg. "Where else could they have gotten the cloning material?"

It was his last gamble. He wanted to know where that child was if it existed. Then he could get rid of her, however he wanted to.

He was no longer sure how he wanted to.

"We got the DNA from her body," Shindo said softly. "They clone the dead on Armstrong. There's a whole industry that does it. I thought you knew that."

She wasn't lying now. He could tell. Still, the news disgusted him. He hadn't known that the Earth Alliance allowed the cloning of the dead anywhere within its borders.

Cloning the dead was forbidden on most worlds where cloning was allowed.

He shrugged, pretending a nonchalance he didn't feel. "You'll never convince the Gyonnese of that. They want you. They want this case. They want to punish Aleyd. They lost an entire generation of children."

"They lost what they call original children," she said. "They weren't even sentient yet."

He clenched his left fist. His right hand hurt too much to move.

"More excuses?" he asked.

"Those larvae divide." Her eyes were bright. She had made these arguments before. "The genetic material is the same in all the subsequent larvae. Just because the originals were killed doesn't mean the individuals are gone."

For someone who was supposed to be smart, she didn't seem to understand the flaws in her argument. He wondered if she would make that argument about human children.

Probably not, since she supposedly lived with a clone.

He said, "You'll never understand the Gyonnese, will you?"

"Why, do you?"

He shook his head.

"You live among them, don't you?" she said. "That's your home, isn't it? On the fringes of the Alliance."

He had gone cold. He had never met anyone like her. Brilliant, but dead inside. He thought brilliant people were the most capable of empathy, but she was proving that theory wrong.

"I'm taking you to them," he said. "This is all too fraught for me. Then I'm going back to non-living things. They don't try to kill me."

"Oh, they will," she said. "That cargo hold of yours is deadly."

"I don't spend a lot of time there," he said.

"It nearly killed me," she said. "I kept some pills for the last of it. What happened to them?"

The cydoleen. He'd left the pills in her pocket. "They're on you."

"Maybe you can get me some medical help and let me take one. I'd like to keep improving. Unless you want me to die before the Gyonnese get me...?"

He sighed. Then he waved his good hand over a nearby console. "Computer, transfer the medical programs to the bridge."

"They're not designed for transfer," the computer responded.

He cursed.

"You only need one of them," she said. "Get whichever one has the capacity to touch. I need someone to set my nose."

Stupid woman. All the medical persona touched. Otherwise they wouldn't work properly.

"I can't swallow otherwise," she said.

"Send the expensive one," he said to the computer. "And have the avatar appear in human form."

"What about equipment?" the computer asked.

"Have a bot bring anything the avatar needs when the avatar asks. And do it quickly."

The computer chirruped as it set about following his commands. Yu leaned toward Shindo, his face only centimeters from her battered one.

"I'm not doing this for you. I'm not helping you in any way. I'm getting my money, and I'm getting out of the human recovery business. If the Gyonnese kill you, fine. If they destroy the Disappeared programs, fine. If they exact revenge on Aleyd, fine. It'll have nothing to do with me."

"It'll have everything to do with you," she said. "Until you found me, this case was dead."

He grinned. The look was mean. "I have news for you, lady. I didn't find you. I just recovered you."

She was frowning as he turned away. She hadn't understood him. He went back to the console.

Then she moaned.

The Gyonnese had found her long before they hired him. Even if she went back, they would come after her again.

Her nightmare was just beginning.

And he couldn't have been happier.

## 18

THE RENDEZVOUS POINT WAS A CLOSED SCIENCE BASE on Io. The base looked like it had been abandoned a hundred years ago. Parts of the structure had fallen down. Other sections were scattered across Io's surface, as if some giant wind had come and shaken the place apart.

The landing had been scary. It was the first time he'd tried to maneuver the ship into a port without benefit of a co-pilot or space-traffic controllers.

But he managed it. When the ship touched the old-fashioned pad which showed he had landed safely by lighting up everything around him, he felt relieved.

He glanced over his shoulder at Rhonda Shindo. She was unconscious. He had kept the bubble around her and cut off the oxygen until she passed out. Then he had given her a shot of something that would make sure she stayed out until he was long gone.

He had packed her into a moving crate which looked like a cold sleep coffin. Her face was still a little bruised. There had been a lot of damage, apparently, or the nano-bots he'd been using hadn't functioned as well as he thought.

Her clothing also had blood on it, and was ripped along one side. He hadn't thought to bring anything else for her, and he really didn't want to change her unconscious form. So he left the ruined clothing on her, hoping that the Gyonnese didn't know enough about humans to care that her clothing was seriously out of order.

He wished now that he'd gotten more than his expenses and the payment to Athenia up front. Normally, he would have contacted the Gyonnese, have the bots deliver her in that coffin, and then leave.

But he couldn't do that. He had to make sure he'd get some payment, and this was the only way. He was afraid the Gyonnese would complain about her physical condition. Technically, he had not violated his agreement with them, but he'd worked with them enough in the past to know how picky they could be, and he worried about that bruised face.

He shut down all of the ship's systems except the essential ones. Then he touched the frame of the coffin, activating its float mechanism. He sent it to the nearest downshaft, and followed, feeling like he was walking to his own death.

He shook off the thought and went to the lower levels of the ship. The science station only had an environment in selected sections and since the landing pad was open to the atmosphere, he had to trust a corridor that automatically attached itself to the side doors.

Considering how old this place was and how damaged, he wasn't going to do that. Instead, he was going to don one of the working environmental suits, let the coffin lead the way, and head out the cargo bay. He would wait until the suit let him know that the environment was suitable before he removed his helmet.

The coffin was already on the lowest bay level when he arrived. He opened a secret compartment off one of the corridors, removed his favorite suit, and put on a thick helmet with a mirrored visor.

According to his suit, the bay he walked through was as contaminated as the hold where he'd originally stashed Shindo. Maybe her face wasn't healing because the bruises there weren't caused by the broken nose. Maybe it wasn't healing because of the contamination.

That was her problem now. He'd given her the pills. She could decide whether or not to take them.

He sighed, then opened the bay doors.

The lights were still on full, revealing a rusted, ruined port, filled with a lot of broken materials and destroyed ships. The landing pad looked like the only patch of ground that wasn't covered with ruined equipment.

The coffin floated toward a sealed doorway. A green light rotated above it, theoretically telling him that everything was clear inside. He'd be able to breathe, he'd be able to stand without gravity boots, he would be warm enough.

Still, he tramped to the airlock doors, feeling like a giant in his suit. There was some Earth level gravity here or his legs wouldn't feel like they were glued to the floor with each step.

Everything felt right—and if he were in one of the lesser suits, he might pull off the helmet the moment the airlock doors opened.

But this suit still hadn't cleared the area. It claimed that the oxygen, carbon dioxide, and carbon monoxide ratios were off. There was also another chemical that the suit didn't have the sophistication to identify.

At that moment, he decided to leave the thing on permanently. He wasn't going to trust that the unknown chemical was safe.

The airlock doors slid open and he stepped inside. The coffin came with him, crowding him as the doors closed behind him. Shindo looked peaceful even though she wasn't. He tried not to look at her. He didn't want to think about her more than he had to.

The interior doors finally opened, and the suit approved. The environment was perfect for him.

Still, he kept the thing on.

A welcoming committee of five Gyonnese ringed the exit from the airlock doors. Yu knew he'd seen all five of these Gyonnese before. In fact, before he had met them, he recognized them from the air vids the Gyonnese used to distribute news. These five Gyonnese weren't leaders of the Gyonnese, but they were the leaders' assistants, famous in their own right among the Gyonnese people.

But Yu didn't know their honorifics and didn't want to guess.

"Where is the woman?" the nearest Gyonnese asked.

"Here," Yu said, putting his hand on the glass coffin.

"You have killed her," the Gyonnese in the center said. "She is worth nothing to us dead."

Yu expected the comment, but hated it anyway. The Gyonnese were quick-tempered and violent. He'd been grabbed by one once: it was like being held by a braided rope made of gooey flesh.

"She's not dead," he said. "She's unconscious. This was the easiest way to move her. I have to warn you. She's very, very difficult."

"We know that," the center Gyonnese said. "If she was not, she would not have killed our children."

Yu sighed, hoping that the visor caught the sound. "I mean hard to handle. You'll need to restrain her from the first. And don't expect her to give into anything. She's a fighter."

He lowered the coffin so that they could see her face.

"That's a bruise." He ran his hand over her face. "I broke her nose trying to keep her from killing me."

"Will she live with that injury?" asked another Gyonnese.

"I had the injury repaired," Yu said. "Even if I hadn't, she could have lived with it. Humans are resilient."

"Then what has disfigured her face if not an injury?" asked yet another Gyonnese.

"The injury disfigured it, and the technique I used to heal it hasn't gotten to that part yet. Also, she was exposed to some contaminants around the time she boarded my ship, so she has some medication to prevent an illness from them."

"I thought humans could remove contaminants," said the center Gyonnese. "Or is that a lie from the Aleyd corporation as well?"

"It's no lie," Yu said, hating discussions with the Gyonnese. They were always circular, but somehow they never ended up where they started. It was as if the discussions did move forward, but in a way he didn't quite understand. "I used the standard method to remove 95% of her contamination. The remaining part is slower, and requires the pills. Make sure she takes them if you want her to remain healthy."

"We do not understand human physiology," the center Gyonnese said. "We cannot be responsible for her care."

"If you like," Yu said, "I can download a medical program that will take care of things for you. I'd have to transfer it from my ship to the original computer in this science facility."

"Do so," the first Gyonnese said.

"However," said the center Gyonnese, "do not expect payment for this program. We would not need it without your negligence."

"I could have kept her from you until she healed," Yu said. "I thought you wanted her quickly."

"We do," the first Gyonnese said.

The center Gyonnese said to the first Gyonnese loudly enough for Yu to hear, "This human is cheating us. We can't even quiz this person to see if she is indeed Rhonda Shindo."

Yu had forgotten that humans looked the same to the Gyonnese, just like Gyonnese looked the same to most humans.

"She is," he said. "She has identification chips in her hands."

"Which we cannot access," the center Gyonnese said.

Then Yu understood. They weren't sure they could open the coffin. So he pressed the side and the lid slid back. The Gyonnese scuttled backwards, swaying as they moved.

Yu grabbed her hand and hung it off the side of the coffin. "Check now."

The Gyonnese stared at her. Their arms flailed behind their backs, fingers touching, obviously communicating in a way he did not understand.

Finally the first Gyonnese scuttled forward. With clear trepidation, he took her hand in his fingers and touched the nearest chip.

He started, then his whiskers spread out wide, and then he dropped her hand as if it had burned him.

"It is she," he said to the others.

A visible shudder ran through him. He excused himself and scuttled into the darkness. A liquid sound, like water filling a bowl, echoed from that spot.

The other Gyonnese bent in the middle, their arms going up.

"Is he all right?" Yu asked.

The Gyonnese rose slowly, as if they were under water.

Yu's heart pounded. He was afraid he had violated some kind of protocol.

Finally, the Gyonnese who hadn't spoken said, "Touching her has made him ill. He will recover, but he will never forget the shame of it."

Yu wasn't sure what his reaction should be. "I didn't know. I could have found another way to verify."

"There is no other way," said the same Gyonnese.

Then the remaining four stared at him as if they expected something.

"Look," Yu said, "I can download the medical program from my ship. She's going to wake up on her own in about four Earth hours. She'll be ready to fight. As I said, make sure she's restrained before that."

"You are certain she is not dead?" the center Gyonnese asked.

"Positive," Yu said, "and if you want, double check with the guy who touched her. Living humans are warm to the touch. She should have been warm. She still is, if someone else wants to verify."

They all scuttled backwards. He was glad they couldn't see inside his visor because he smiled at their reaction.

"She is warm." The first Gyonnese came out of the darkness. His skin had turned an orange-yellow.

"See?" Yu said. "All I need is my payment. Then I'll send the download and leave you to do whatever you're going to do."

"No," the center Gyonnese said.

Yu froze. He'd expected some argument, but not an outright no.

"I delivered her," Yu said. "You promised payment upon receipt. I trusted you. I didn't even take a deposit, and this woman cost me. She murdered my partner. See why I'm warning you?"

"We have no proof that your partner is dead," the center Gyonnese said.

"I can give you his body," Yu snapped. "You want it? I don't know what to do with it."

Four of them scuttled even farther back, but the center one stayed in position.

"We shall pay half."

"Half?" Yu asked. He hadn't expected this. The Gyonnese had always been fair until now.

"She is damaged. We know nothing of your kind. She might live until you are far from here, and then she will die. We need her alive for court."

"She's fine," Yu said.

"You have told us she's ill."

"I also told you it was nothing major." But had he? Bruised meant that she was fine to humans, but what did it mean to Gyonnese? And the contamination. He'd explained the 95% but not how severe the 5% was.

"We have no external verification for that."

"You'll have the medical program," Yu said.

"Which you will give us," the center Gyonnese said. "We cannot trust it."

They had a point, but he wasn't going to concede it. "I want full payment."

"You will get the second half when she appears in court," the center Gyonnese said.

"Pay me three-quarters," Yu said. "I've lost my assistant."

"Half," the center Gyonnese said.

"I'll take her away," Yu said.

"Half." The center Gyonnese took his long arms and folded them across his body. He had clearly negotiated with humans before.

Yu had already negotiated a full price higher than anything he'd ever received from the Gyonnese. Maybe they'd figured that out. Half would still be more than he'd ever made from them.

"Half," he said, "if you pay me the rest after she wakes."

"You are not staying," the center Gyonnese said.

"Nope," Yu said. "I'm going to get my hand repaired. When it's done, I'll come back, and you give me the rest."

"When we take her to court."

"No," Yu said. "If I don't get the second payment in the next few Earth days, I'm taking her now. You get nothing."

He heard a shushering sound, and realized that was the other Gyonnese talking softly, without benefit of the amplification device.

Finally the center Gyonnese said, "Half. The second payment will come within one Earth week."

That was about how long it would take him to find an adequate medical facility, to have the repair, and then to return.

"Fine," Yu said. "I want the first half now."

"Done," the center Gyonnese said. "You owe us a medical program."

"You'll get it as soon as I return to the ship."

"How do we take custody of the woman?" the center Gyonnese said.

Yu pressed the side of the coffin. "Where do you want it?"

"We want it to follow us," the center Gyonnese said.

"As soon as I verify payment, I'll program that," Yu said.

Instantly his links hummed. They had been blocking most of the nearby network. He quickly scanned the account he'd given them when they made the deal, and then he tapped part of the coffin.

"She's all yours," he said. "Good luck with her. You'll need it."

# 19

And finally, Yu was free. He hurried back to his ship, closing all the doors behind him and setting double locking protocols. He used an emergency voice command to power up the systems before he got to the bridge, and he didn't even remove his environmental suit as he moved through the ship.

He stopped at decon and went into the machine himself. He left the environmental suit in a secondary decon unit.

Neither units recorded any problems, but he still felt dirty.

He knew that was because of the job.

The job, the injuries, the loss of Nafti. All the mistakes Yu had made. He almost regretted leaving the woman behind. She would find no sympathy from the Gyonnese. But they wouldn't kill her.

No matter how much she deserved it.

He got to the bridge and sank into the pilot's chair. He had to be careful as he took off because he had no help. If he was going to make more mistakes this was where he would do it.

The ship rose quickly and the lights on the pad went out. He didn't breathe deeply, though, until he was outside Io's orbit and on his way out of the solar system.

Shindo was with the Gyonnese. And if he didn't register his flight plan with anyone, no one would come after him for a while.

He had his onboard computer search for a base outside this sector that specialized in human hand repair.

It took a while for the ship to locate one, but when it did, it gave him the information. He programmed it into the navigational system.

Then he set the ship on autopilot and went into his cabin for a long, much deserved rest.

# 20

THE SHIP WOKE HIM IN SOME WEIRD ASTEROID BELT that didn't show up on any of the charts. The ship didn't believe the autopilot was enough to avoid collision.

He felt that it was, but stirred himself anyway. He had some other business that had to be completed here.

He went onto the bridge and called up the readings for the belt. The asteroids were closer together than in any other belt he'd traveled through. No wonder the ship wanted extra guidance.

He waited until they found a fairly large gap between the rocks and ordered a full stop. Then he ran a hand over his face. He was still tired. Deep down exhausted, in fact, and sick of himself. He knew this would only make him feel worse.

He could have had the bots do it.

But he was having enough trouble living with himself these last few days. Shrugging this job off on the bots would only make him feel worse.

He went to medical lab and stared at Nafti. Nafti's skin had gone a horrible whitish color that showed the veins in his face and hands. His eyes, which no one had bothered to close (which *Yu* hadn't bothered to close), had clouded over.

Nafti didn't look human any more.

But that didn't excuse what happened or the way Yu had treated him. Yu had never given Nafti any respect, even though he had hired Nafti for his strength and experience.

Yu could use that strength now. The trek to the smallest cargo bay would be a difficult one.

Yu ran a hand over his hair. He didn't even know what to say over Nafti's body or if he should say anything. He didn't even know if Nafti left a family behind. He had no idea if there was someone to contact about Nafti's death. He'd never had Nafti fill out any forms.

Yu wasn't even sure if Janus Nafti was the man's real name.

Yu sighed. Then he hit buttons on the side of the diagnostic table, unhooking it from the floor and giving it wheels instead of feet. He tucked Nafti's arms on his torso and grimaced. The corpse was ice-cold. At least it wasn't in rigor any longer. Yu would have hated having those arms hanging over the side, bumping into corners as he wheeled the table out of the medical lab.

It took longer than he expected to get to the cargo level. He had to go around some tight corners, and once the wheels got stuck. Yu struggled, but eventually freed them.

He didn't want to remove Nafti sooner than he had to.

Using his good hand on the back of the cart, Yu pushed the body into the smallest cargo bay. This bay was empty of everything. Yu rarely used it, except to jettison cargo that he didn't want. And since he didn't want valuable items disappearing into space, he just made sure nothing stayed in that bay at all.

He pushed the diagnostic table into the bay. It was cold, with unpainted metallic walls and a matching floor. Not much to look at, and certainly not enough to pass as a ceremonial transition spot from one life to the next—if, indeed, Nafti had believed in the kind of thing.

Nafti would go out into space unprotected, which seemed wrong, given how much Nafti wanted to protect that huge body of his.

Yu pushed the table to the exterior door. Then he looked at the man he'd worked with for years and hadn't really known.

"I'm sorry," Yu said again, and used his one good hand to shove Nafti off the table.

The body landed so hard that the table bounced. Yu winced. He didn't look down. He didn't want to see if he had done any more damage.

Instead, he grabbed the edge of the table and pulled it behind him as he scurried out of the cargo bay.

Then he sealed the interior door and opened the exterior door to space.

He closed his eyes and counted to two hundred. Then he closed the exterior door.

With luck, Nafti would float out here with the asteroids, and no one would ever find him. He would show up as another bit of space debris on other ships' sensors.

Space debris.

Yu shook his head and opened his eyes. Then he stood on tiptoe and peered through the window into the bay.

No body lay on the floor.

Nafti was gone as if he had never been.

# 21

The medical base Yu's sensors had found doubled as a space port. The base had been built by one of the corporations as it expanded throughout the known universe, but that corporation had long ago sold it to a medical company that specialized in delicate procedures.

People came from all over to receive new limbs or to get high-end augmentations. The enhancements that were standard on places like Earth were discouraged here. If someone wanted a prettier face, they could go to some medical base in Earth's solar system.

If they wanted to upgrade their hand or augment their sense of smell to equal that of a dog's, they came here. This base improved on the human condition; it didn't repair the human condition.

Normally, Yu would have gone somewhere that specialized in repair. He didn't need a high-end hand. But this was the most reputable medical base the farthest from Earth, and it would be hard to track him here.

In fact, the base's information stressed privacy. No one would ever know if a piano player improved his dexterity or a chef upgraded his sense of taste.

Or if a Recovery Man who—by this point—was probably running from authorities got a new and better hand, replacing the one he'd damaged delivering a kidnapped woman to the Gyonnese.

The medical facilities were stunning—a luxury in and of themselves. He felt like he was going into a spa instead of an examination room. Everything was calibrated to his tastes—the spicy scented air, the goldish-brown lighting, the subtle reds and oranges on the walls. The medical personnel spoke in hushed tones, probably because someone had noted the Gyonnese influence on his ship, and they treated the wounds as if they were fresh instead of days old.

After intensive examinations and a lot of consultations, the surgeons here told him that the medical avatar had been right; his hand could not be saved. He would receive an artificial hand which was, as Shindo had so snidely observed, much better than his own.

He received medication, instructions, and a helper who would see him through the latter stages of the procedure. At the moment, all he had to do was choose the make and model of the hand he wanted. He was stunned to realize he could afford several hundred of the high-end models, not because they were cheap, but because the Gyonnese had paid the first half of the last quoted price—the one that he had inflated beyond measure. He figured they would pay half of the first quoted price, and cheat him of the rest.

They were being fairer than he expected.

So he ordered the most expensive hand. It looked like all the others to him, but it had features that the others didn't have, from various external chips that worked with his links to internal mechanisms that allowed him to set the hand's strength depending on the task before him. He could push a finger-sized hole in the hull of his ship if he wanted to or touch a goblet without shattering the crystal.

They offered to replace both hands so that his strengths would balance. He knew that a lot of clients did such things, but he wasn't going to replace body parts unless he needed it.

Part of him was appalled he had to replace this one.

The doctors had him start the procedure immediately. They were afraid of infection in the damaged hand. So they unceremoniously cut it off.

He felt no pain—the initial injury had been a lot more painful than the loss of the hand—but it shocked him to look at the stump. They had sealed the skin but they wanted him in the most sterile parts of the medical wing.

The risk of infection was too great to have him go to the recreation area or back to his ship.

So he had to find a way to pass the time.

Drinking was out. He didn't want to view the entertainment holos and the live entertainments in the medical unit didn't interest him. His external links had been disconnected—too many false emergency calls from links happened during surgery—and he had shut off many of the other links.

He didn't want to be traceable.

But before he went completely off the grid, he had to check his messages. He wanted that final payment from the Gyonnese.

The message center of the medical wing looked oddly alien. Each message unit had its own privacy booth that rose around the equipment like a pointed egg. The booths were opaque, but transparent enough so that medical personnel could see if the person inside was in some sort of distress.

As he went inside, he felt like he was going into some kind of cocoon.

The privacy booth didn't seem that sterile. The opaque interior light made him nervous and exposed. All he could see through the walls were moving shadows.

He cradled his right arm to his chest, wishing he already had the new hand.

Once he settled inside, he ran his own diagnostic, checking for tracers that attached themselves to messages and stole the information.

Just as he finished, he'd gotten an urgent notice on his own links. The notice had come from the message center, saying he had a communication waiting.

He used his personal code to call up the message.

One of the Gyonnese filled the screen in front of him. Its whiskers moved, then an automated voice with a flat tone said, "You have cheated us. We tried to stop the original payment and could not. You will not get your second payment."

"What?" Yu said, but Gyonnese did not respond. The message was as automated as the translator's voice.

"The woman is dead."

Dead? Yu blinked in astonishment. There was no way she could be dead. She wasn't that badly injured.

He wondered if the Gyonnese were trying to cheat him. But cheating wasn't something they usually did.

Had she played a trick on them?

The message continued. "The medical program you sent confirms it," the Gyonnese said. "You told us she lived and took our money. You will get no more from us. You will never work for the Gyonnese again. Do not appeal this decision. The woman's employer has placed notification all over the Alliance that she has been kidnapped. If you appeal, we will prove that you acted alone. Do not contact us again."

And with that, the image winked out.

Yu ran his remaining hand over his face. Maybe the Gyonnese had killed her. Or maybe she had died from the contamination.

The contamination. Something niggled at his brain.

He ran the message again. The automatic voice was flat, but the Gyonnese was angry. Its eyes widened and its whiskers moved rapidly as it spoke.

They hadn't killed her—or if they had, they had done so accidentally.

He hadn't realized she was so sick. If he'd known, he would have sent the good medical program, not the cheap one.

And he had given her the pills.

The pills.

Cydoleen.

He closed his eyes, trying to remember how many were in that bottle. He remembered the weight of it, the way it felt solid in his hand.

There had been more than enough cydoleen to kill her if she took it all at once.

She must have poisoned herself.

He wondered: was that an admission of guilt on her part? Or was it fear of facing the courts alone, without corporate support?

Yu sighed and shook his head. He would never know.

But he would always wonder. Why would a woman who claimed to love a child—even if it was a Sixth—kill herself? Was what she was facing from the Gyonnese that bad?

Yu made himself stop thinking about her. He had to focus on himself now.

The fact that the Gyonnese wouldn't pay any more didn't bother him. He had enough for the new hand, some ship upgrades, and a year without working—and that was just from this job. The remaining money in his various accounts would last him a decade or more even if he didn't work again.

He might be able to make that stretch.

Yu played the message one more time, recorded it onto his links, and shook his head.

The Gyonnese had never understood how the Alliance legal system worked. Just because they said they knew nothing about the kidnapping didn't mean that there wasn't proof of their involvement.

Yu had worried about this case, so he had kept everything—and not just on his own system. He had it on his ship, in one of his accounts, and on a back-up network that he occasionally used.

If the Gyonnese turned him in, they'd suffer the consequences. He'd make sure of it.

He double-checked to make sure he had a copy of the Gyonnese message, then he deleted the message from the private server.

Then he stared at his damaged arm. Maybe he'd get some kind of sterile sling or something to put over the wrist. He needed a drink—and not the crappy stuff they had in the medical wing.

He needed a drink and maybe some companionship and some kind of entertainment.

He needed to explore the rest of the facility so that he wouldn't have to think of the woman he'd given them, and wonder how she'd died.

With his good hand, he pulled the door open, and froze. People surrounded his booth. They all wore silver uniforms with gray logos and badge numbers along the sleeve.

Earth Alliance Police.

He willed himself to be calm. He'd run into them before, and survived. If he kept his wits, he'd survive this one.

The woman nearest him had ginger hair and skin so dark it made the hair glow. Her eyes were a silver that matched her uniform.

"Hadad Yu?" she asked.

"Yes," he said, since there was no point in denying it.

"You're under arrest."

For any one of a thousand crimes. He wasn't going to guess. "I don't have to go with you unless you tell me what the charges are."

"Kidnapping," she said. "Transporting a human through the Alliance with the intention of selling her. Related theft and assault charges. And attempted murder."

"Murder?" he blurted. They couldn't have found Nafti's body. It floated in the vastness of space between here and Io. There wasn't even proof that Nafti had been on his ship; Yu had cleared all that off.

Nor was there obvious proof he'd held Rhonda Shindo either.

"I didn't try to murder anyone," he said.

"A young woman named Talia Shindo disagrees," the officer said. "Now, would you like to stand or do we get to drag you out of there?"

He held out his damaged arm. "I'm here for medical treatment."

"And you'll get it, in the prison wing. We'll leave as soon as they've grafted something on there."

"I ordered a hand. I paid for it."

"Fine," she said. "You're still under arrest."

"What am I supposed to have kidnapped?" he asked.

"A woman named Rhonda Shindo on Callisto."

The Gyonnese had turned him in anyway, the bastards. They were vicious when they were denied their revenge.

"If I tell you a few things, will you let me go?" he asked.

"Not with charges like this," she said. "But you can see what an attorney will do for you. Do you have something to bargain with?"

"I always have something to bargain with," he said as he stood and let them lead him away.

# 22

The attorney Yu hired was brilliant. Not only did he get Yu cleared of all charges, he got rid of the evidence too.

And did all of it using Yu's one and only bargaining chip: The Black Fleet.

The Fleet owed Yu a favor. He concocted one and requested a meet.

Then he set up his ship so that a shadow version of himself sat at the helm. He removed the ship's computer and replaced it with another, so the authorities couldn't track all of his movements.

And then he gave the authorities the ship, contaminants and all.

Yu wasn't the one who was going to meet the Black Fleet.

The Earth Alliance Police were, armed with the device the Fleet had given Yu, confessing to stealing the flowering fidelia. He had a hunch the Alliance would find a lot more on them.

He was sure the Alliance *had* a lot more on them.

Not that it mattered to him.

All that mattered to him was learning how to use his new arm, buying a new ship, and figuring out his future.

His future was the hardest part.

He was tired of working hard and gaining nothing. He had put three years into the flowering fidelia, and all it had gotten him was the enmity of Athenia, a near loss of his life savings, and a willingness to break all his rules.

Not to mention the worst part: two deaths that he felt responsible for—Nafti's and Shindo's.

And then there was the daughter. The Sixth, as the Gyonnese would call her. The one who had pressed the charges against Yu.

Because Yu had spent three years tracking down the flowering fidelia, because he had lost it to the Fleet, because he had decided to take a job he didn't believe in, Talia Shindo's life was ruined.

She no longer had a mother. She didn't really have an identity either.

Sometimes, at night when he couldn't sleep from the pain of the procedures, he kept hearing her plaintive voice. That tiny "What?" after he had cruelly told her she was hatched.

He wondered if she thought of that. He wondered how she had dealt with it.

He wondered where she was now.

He would never know.

He didn't dare know. He couldn't track her down. That would violate his agreement with the Earth Alliance Police.

They made him promise not to break Earth Alliance laws again.

It was a condition of his release.

In the past, he would have laughed at that condition. But he was no longer the same man.

For the first time in years, the universe was open to him.

But he was no longer thinking of it as a place full of things. It was a place full of creatures—sentient beings with lives of their own, problems of their own, loves of their own. Creatures he had never gotten to know.

He had been afraid to get involved with others, afraid they would hurt him.

And one of them had. He had a new hand to show for it.

But he had hurt her worse.

And her daughter—her innocent cloned daughter— was paying for all of it.

Yu couldn't make up for what he had done to Talia Shindo. But he could make sure he didn't do anything like that again.

And the first way he could do that was to stay out of the Recovery business. To live an honest life, whatever that meant.

He wasn't sure how to do it, but he could learn anything. If he could remove a flowering fidelia from its colesis tree without killing the tree, the vine, or the flower, he could do anything.

He just had to concentrate on it.

And he had to think through the consequences, something he had never done before.

Everything he did affected someone else.

Strange that he had to live half of his life before realizing it.

But he knew it now.

He'd learned that lesson.

And it changed everything.

# ABOUT THE AUTHOR

INTERNATIONAL BESTSELLING WRITER KRISTINE Kathryn Rusch has won or been nominated for every major award in the science fiction field. She has won Hugos for editing *The Magazine of Fantasy & Science Fiction* and for her short fiction. She has also won the *Asimov's Science Fiction Magazine* Readers Choice Award six times, as well as the Anlab Award from *Analog Magazine*, *Science Fiction Age* Readers Choice Award, the Locus Award, and the John W. Campbell Award. Her standalone sf novel, *Alien Influences*, was a finalist for the prestigious Arthur C. Clarke Award. *Io9* said her Retrieval Artist series featured one of the top ten science fiction detectives ever written. She writes a second sf series, the Diving Universe series, as well as a fantasy series called The Fey. She also writes mystery, romance and fantasy novels, occasionally using the pen names Kris DeLake, Kristine Grayson and Kris Nelscott.

## The Retrieval Artist Series:

21732796R00094

Made in the USA
Lexington, KY
26 March 2013